Stray Voltage

Stray Voltage

Eugenie Doyle

FRONT STREET

Asheville, North Carolina

Library of Congress Cataloging-in-Publication Data

Doyle, Eugenie
Stray voltage / by Eugenie Doyle.
p. cm.
Summary: After his mother leaves to start a new
life elsewhere, eleven-year-old Ian sees changes
in his father and in their failing Vermont
farm, changes that cannot be ignored.
ISBN 1-886910-86-3 (alk. paper)
[1. Parent and child—Fiction.
2. Farm life—Vermont—Fiction.
3. Vermont—Fiction.] I. Title.
PZ7.D7745 St 2002
[Fic]-dc21   2002069252

Thanks to my parents who read to me when I was little and told me great stories. And thanks to my son Silas for his acrostic:

Summer
Is
Like
A
Song

Stray Voltage

Current Events

Ian Daley printed CHRISTMAS LIST on the back of an old grain bill. Underneath he wrote, "Subscription, Green Mountain World and News." He stared at the words. *Subscription* ... a spelling word. What an idiotic present for an eleven-year-old kid!

He left his pathetic list on the mess of a kitchen counter, certain that neither Dad nor Aunt Julie would notice it, since they hadn't even asked him what he wanted. He hoped they would buy the stupid paper just the same, whether for him or not, for Christmas or not. Mrs. Worth said he needed a regular supply of news articles for Current Events homework. Mrs. Worth was pretty much the only bright light around this holiday season.

His mother probably thought she was Santa Claus kicking off Christmas with a bang when she gave him a kitten in early November. She knew he liked cats and that he'd had his heart broken twice in two years when his favorites disappeared, dead from coydogs or trucks on Route 14. That was how Mom put it: his heart was broken. She always called sad things "heartbreaking." He'd missed those cats, especially the first one, Golden Guernsey, so much that it did hurt his chest right where she said his heart was. But now he wondered, what did she know about his heart?

The new kitten had appeared beside his bed that morning asleep in a canning jar box lined with Ian's old baby quilt. A note jutting out read:

Dear Ian, here's
a little early present.
I have to go away
awhile.
Might not be back
by Christmas.
This little guy
will be good company.
Love ya, Mom
P.S. Don't worry. Aunt Julie will help out.

The kitten was tiny, black with a long white tail wrapped around like a halo; it slept soundly with a fragile rise and fall of breath. Very cute, incredibly cute, but at first he couldn't even touch it. He'd gone through the farmhouse calling, "Mom, Mom." He'd tried the same thing in the barn across the road, but his older brother Ray said, "Shut up, she's gone. Whadya expect? If you don't want to see Dad madder than usual, just shut up and help with chores."

By the time the milking was done and Ian had returned to his room, his head throbbed and his stomach was cramped into a ball. He finally scooped the kitten up, pressing the fur to his cheek. His mother was wrong. This handful wasn't enough to be good company. He couldn't bother to think of a name except Little Guy.

Now, a month later, Mom, true to her dumb word, hadn't returned, and Dad, true to Ray's word, wouldn't talk about her, or blew up if Ian tried to. He and Ray had gotten one note on the back of a "Rock of Ages" granite quarry postcard sent to Aunt Julie and handed over:

Boys, I'm at Uncle Jack's.
Julie says
you're doing good.
Love ya, Mom

No, Ian didn't care much about Christmas—just the paper, please, for school. He'd had enough surprises.

"What's this?" Aunt Julie asked as she waved a soggy scrap of paper in Ian's direction. Her fingers were speckled with soap bubbles from washing the supper pots. "You want the newspaper for Christmas? Warren, you got a strange boy here."

Ian's father slouched on the sofa, his eyes squinting at *Monday Night Football*. He grunted, "Which one?"

Ian tried to focus on his homework sheets, spread among other papers on the kitchen table. "I need it for school, for doing Current Events."

"Ian needs the paper for homework, Warren, did you hear what he said? Don't you get the paper?"

"Not anymore," Ian said.

"Warren!" Aunt Julie yelled over the drone of the football commentator.

"What the hell?" Dad sat up, bleary-eyed, gruff. A bear, thought Ian.

"Ian needs the newspaper for homework. He wants it for Christmas. What the hell kind of present? You got to do some preparation here. Only got two weeks."

Ian's father snorted something between a laugh and a grunt. "Right," he said, settling back into the cushions. "We already get the damn newspaper. Your sister had to have it. Can't live without Dear old Abby and the friggin' crossword puzzle, which she couldn't ever finish anyway."

"Jeez, Dad, there's a kid here. You got to call it a blankety-blank crossword puzzle." Ray's pimply face looked up from the TV, smirking.

Ian stopped writing. He wished Dad wouldn't insult Mom, but he was mad at her too. He pictured her driving from her hideout at Uncle Jack's in Barre, where, according to Aunt Julie, she'd gone to "think," up to the blue newspaper tube near the mailbox in the dark of dawn before even Dad was up, and robbing the newspaper. Would she? Outraged, he looked up for sympathy from Aunt Julie.

She had finished cleaning the kitchen and was pulling a blue toque down over her ears. With her reddish hair covered she looked so much like Mom he almost cried out, *No!* First Mom left, then maybe she'd started coming in the night to steal what he needed for school. And now Aunt Julie had covered her hair, which was the only physical feature that distinguished her from her twin. It used to puzzle Ian that people got them mixed up. He saw only how different they were: Mom warm and smiling, Aunt Julie cool and serious. But just now Ian was shocked to see them turn into a single person, and it wasn't the one he wanted.

"Dad, you just haven't paid the bills," Ray yelled over Ian's head into the living room. He had wandered into the kitchen and stood with a box of crackers in one hand, a fistful of envelopes from the jumble on the table in the other. "Here's like two or three from *World and News*. Funny, they don't give it out for free."

"Smartass," Dad grumbled. Ian could hear the thuds and thumps of Dad stuffing the stove with wood chunks for the night. But he didn't sound mad at Ray. Ray could get away with saying all kinds of stuff to Dad. Why didn't Ray tell him to go get Mom? "I'm going to bed," Dad said. The damper on the stove squeaked and Dad's boots clumped up the stairs.

Mom always made everyone take their barn boots off in the mudroom. He and Ray still did, and Aunt Julie did, of course, when she came over. Not Dad. When Mom came home, she'd freak at what Dad had tracked in.

Before Aunt Julie closed the kitchen door and headed home to her place across Jiggles Brook, she poked her head, still looking weirdly like Mom, back inside.

"Boys," she said, "come for haircuts after school tomorrow. My present. You both're looking awful shaggy."

Ian lay in bed that night shivering. It wasn't any colder than usual, but his feet felt numb, and he curled up to warm them with his hands.

Ian and his father had gone to the barn for chores at about four o'clock. The barn's red front looked on fire from the sun setting behind them, behind the house. But he had no time to search for the sunset and see what it might be doing to the clouds. His mother would always stroll around the side of the house and say something like, "Look, Ian, every night the colors are different." His father had stamped off the porch and struck out fast, no dilly-dallying.

Ian locked his eyes onto the toe tips of his black rubber pull-ons and tried to will them to match the stride of his father's worn, cracked boots. Cruddy old tires, Ian thought. How could Dad go so fast on them? When he crossed with his mother he used to wish she would slow down; today he only wanted to keep up. If he pushed each leg a little harder he could leap it into place with a slapping sound just short of Dad's.

"What are you jumping around for? You're like the damn cows! Save your energy. You'll need it," Dad said.

"I know." He couldn't reach the milkhouse door before his father and felt silly scrambling in after him, large leaps reduced to shuffling scampers so as to make the step before the door swung shut.

Once they were inside, his father barked, "Set up the milkers," and disappeared through the swinging doors into the stable. Ian sighed and could see his breath. Same old job. The steel pails and milking machine claws were ice cold, and their clanging hurt his ears. At least when Mom was here, he had company: they first set up the milkroom equipment, then went through the stable doors together to the warm cows.

During chores that night Ian thought he felt the stray voltage that made the cows dance around. He'd paused his shovel in midswing of the sawdust and watched the cows fidget. Tails flicked, hips rocked as their hooves treaded side to side. His own feet began to hurt then, like when the porch is hot in summer, and he hopped from one foot to the other. Or maybe his feet were just cold.

Later, in bed, he fell asleep wondering.

When Ian got off the bus the next day the blank windows of his house stared darkly at him like big eyes. He was almost glad to have somewhere to go, even if it was only for a cold half-mile walk through the hayfield down to the brook and along the gravel driveway to Aunt Julie's.

Ray had reminded him at breakfast not to forget the haircut but said Ian would have to go alone. Ray had basketball practice. No surprise. Since Mom left, Ray bossed him around and did whatever he wanted. It showed how little Aunt Julie knew, to think Ray would come. He never went anywhere with Ian if he could help it. Now that he was sixteen and had his license and the use of Dad's Ranger pickup, he didn't even ride the bus with Ian. In the fall Mom had asked Ray to take Ian places, and she probably would have made Ray go for the haircut, since it was supposed to be a present from Aunt Julie, but she wasn't here, was she?

No, Ray would show up at five o'clock for chores the way he always did. Basketball, chores, or driving around, that was where you could find Ray. In the house just to eat and sleep.

Ian went up the porch steps, through the mudroom, then the kitchen. The smell hit him before he saw the small brown plop on the wooden floor in front of the stove. Second time this week.

It stunk sour and out of place, unlike plain old manure in the barn. Ian began to taste the greasy fries he'd had for lunch. He wanted to leave his backpack and run to Aunt Julie's, but just then Little Guy yawned and stretched and wobbled over to him from a pile of old towels on the floor. He climbed onto Ian's foot and batted at frayed denim from a rip in the knee of his jeans. Ian scooped him up. "You know better than that," he said and held the soft fur to his cheek for a minute, just long enough to get an earful of purring before Little Guy swatted at his ear and Ian remembered how annoying he was.

Thanks a lot, Mom, he thought. Some present when you have to feed it and clean it up and Dad doesn't even think it should be inside. No one could find the litter box from their last kitten, so Ian was using the cardboard box Mom left. Even filled with sawdust and with the poop scooped out all the time, it got wet and smelly. Maybe that was why Little Guy used the floor. Ray told Ian to leave him in the barn like Chloe and the wild black cat, but Ian knew they'd eat him alive, he was so tiny.

"You're glad to see me, aren't you?" Ian squeezed him, hard, and set him on the sofa while he dumped out his books. Then he stuffed Little Guy in the backpack for the trip to Aunt Julie's. Hurriedly he wiped up the mess and set off.

Probably with his eyes closed Ian could walk to the "home place," the next farm down, where his mother and Aunt Julie grew up with their big brothers, Jack and Charlie. It sat off the main road, down a long dirt driveway. Aunt Julie's scissors sign, HAIRCARE CLASSIQUE, was posted on the main road above her mailbox. Ian didn't take the main road; he cut through the fields, hard with crunchy grass stubble, the path they always took.

Aunt Julie didn't keep cows anymore—she sold them after Gramma and Grampa LeClaire died—but the home place still seemed like a farm. A little yellow house and big gray barn. Ian's family hayed these fields. This barn held hay that they used or Aunt Julie sold, depending on the year. Behind the barn's south wall were Aunt Julie's three hives of Italian honeybees, and the garden, her peaceful garden. In the summer Ian came here a lot with his mother to weed, to help Aunt Julie pick peas or cucumbers, or just to sit while the grownups talked. About problems: Dad and electricity.

Last summer they came so often that Ian, watching from the garden's safe border, got to know the bees' habits: their grumpy hum on cloudy days, their joyful or crazy stunt-pilot flights on sunny days, the way they got blown about by wind and landed wobbly on the bottom board, the way workers hauled dead bees from the hive entrance and pushed them over the edge of the board onto the grass.

Once Aunt Julie gave him a pair of long-bladed clippers like a huge version of her haircutting scissors. She told him to snip the tall grass in front of the hives so the bees could land at home more easily.

"Don't I need a veil?" he'd asked hopefully. He'd seen her work with the hives, removing frames of honey, checking for drone comb or queen cells, reversing the heavy boxes she called "supers." Why she had to do each chore he didn't exactly know, but she always dressed for the jobs in a hat with a thick, dark veil covering her face and neck, long sleeves and pants, light-colored and worn leather gloves up over her elbows. She carried a small, smoking canister with a squeeze box attached, and puffed smoke into the hives as a greeting. It calmed the bees, or scared them into eating too much honey and becoming too logy to sting. Or the smoke obscured their signals and they didn't get the message that they had a visitor. Ian wasn't too sure about just what the smoke did, since Aunt Julie changed her story from time to time. But he'd never seen her get stung.

Aunt Julie laughed as if he were silly to ask for the veil, but she brought it and the long gloves. Even with them on, he felt wary of the whizzing insects and clipped the grass quickly.

Mom smiled at him but kept her distance safely among the peas.

The hives were motionless now, white double-decker

boxes. Ian knew it was too cold for the bees to fly. They were clustered inside on honeycombs surrounding their queen and eating honey to keep warm. According to Aunt Julie, they kept their cluster around 50°F—warmer than the barn! Ian wished he could see inside the hives, because they sure looked dead and empty. The only signs of life were faint tan spatterings on the snow near the entrances and across the front boards of the hives. From cleansing flights. Ian knew it meant the bees were alive and keeping the hive clean. They never messed in their house. "Little Guy," he said to the pack on his back, "I wish you were more like a bee."

He walked to the side of one hive and pressed his ear to the cold white paint. No sound. Cautiously he pulled off a mitten and rapped on the side of the upper story close to where his ear still pressed. He knocked again. A faint hum broke the utter quiet, and he smiled. Quickly he glanced toward Aunt Julie's workroom in the front of her house. She wouldn't want him bothering the bees like some devilish bear or skunk. She kept a gun for those.

The smell of her haircutting room—her "salon," she called it—bit his nose as he came in jangling the string of bells that hung from the door. Compared to the sweet cold outside, the hair perfume was sharp and over-whelming.

Aunt Julie stood at the movable chair looking at him

by way of the mirror and fussing with Mrs. Stillwater's tight gray curls. The room smelled of ladies. Aunt Julie's own hair was brighter red than last night, as if she had washed it with fire. She didn't look like Mom now. Mom's hair was brown like his and soft to touch. Aunt Julie always offered to color it. "Why so dull, Mariette? You don't have to look plain just 'cause we were born that way." Ian hated when she talked to Mom like that, as though she were the boss and Mom a little kid. Mom said Aunt Julie was only twenty-one minutes older, for crying out loud!

Mrs. Stillwater smiled at him as she got up. She rummaged in her purse and offered a candycane, small and cracked in its clear wrapper. Cracked or not, it looked good and he thanked her.

"Sit down, what you waiting for?" Aunt Julie looked at him as though she were sorry she'd offered this present. She checked her watch, even though there was a clock on the wall saying 4:15.

Ian climbed into the chair and slid the pack from his back onto his lap.

"What'd ya do? Bring your homework?" She snapped the plastic smock and draped it around Ian.

With his arms and legs covered and only his face and stringy brown hair staring from the mirror, Ian suddenly felt stupid and out of place. He looked at the huge tub of bristly pink rollers, bottle after bottle of shampoo and conditioner, can after can of Hair Net. He looked at the bulbous hairdryer behind him and the low table spread with hairdo magazines and the same *Bride* magazine he'd looked at last summer while waiting for his mother; he couldn't believe he'd ever liked coming here. The familiar tattered sign attached to the lower corner of the mirror before him seemed to be Aunt Julie's motto: *Beekeeping is a business that requires the greatest amount of attention to the smallest details. The good beekeeper is generally more or less cranky.—C. P. Dadant.*

Ian did have to give Aunt Julie credit: she seemed to know herself pretty well.

Neither he nor Aunt Julie said a word, and he closed his eyes as she squirted water on his head. Without his mother as a link to all this, he promised himself no more haircuts here, ever. He would cut his own with the cow clippers in the barn the way Dad did once. He'd go to the barber shop like a normal kid.

Little Guy began mewing softly and Ian fumbled to open an air vent in the pack for him.

"When was the last time you washed your hair?" Aunt Julie asked. "Even once since ...? A long time, I bet. Doesn't that man notice anything? Not a damn thing."

Ian didn't feel he should answer any of these questions, since she seemed content answering them herself. As she scooted him to the wash sink, she asked, "What the hell you got under there?" The smock bulged out in front and the mewing was louder. "That kitten?"

Ian nodded.

"Well, take him out. Charger's in the house."

Ian had forgotten about Charger, Aunt Julie's big German shepherd, who usually jumped all over him. "Is he sick?"

"Yah, or he'd be barking his head off. That kitten will be sick too if you smother it in there."

"That's okay, he's okay." Ian didn't want to lose the warm patch on his lap or to bear Aunt Julie's anger if the kitten misbehaved. He pictured cleaning cat poop off those bristly rollers. Jeez, even Aunt Julie's bees were housetrained.

"Can I have a buzz?" He spoke up suddenly from the wash chair with his neck crooked back painfully and her hands scrubbing lather into his head. He wanted suddenly to be done with anything smacking of hair fuss. Ray always got a buzz, usually at the barber Dad went to once a year in Greensbrook.

"What? Now? After I got you all wet?" Aunt Julie's forehead had a million lines like plow furrows between her eyebrows.

Ian just looked up at her and pretended he hadn't said a word.

"You want to look like handsome Ray? Well, you won't anyway. He looks like my brothers, Jack and Charlie. You take after your dad."

Everyone called Ray handsome, but it hadn't really occurred to Ian to want that. He just wanted to get away from Aunt Julie and this haircut, another stupid present.

"I just hope you don't get electrocuted by the clippers, you being all wet." Aunt Julie met Ian's worried eyes in the mirror. "Relax, I'm kidding."

Just before he left feeling taller and lightheaded, Aunt Julie handed him two envelopes, one addressed *To Ray* and one *To Ian*. She nodded when he asked, "From Mom?" and then went back to sweeping her floor.

"When did you see her?" he asked.

"When I go to Barre, shopping, whatever." She shrugged. Ian hated her, that she was still sweeping his stupid hair. She shook her red head and muttered, "You will too. She's just got some growing up to do."

On the way home he opened his envelope and found a glossy card: a Christmas scene, Mary, Joseph, baby Jesus on some hay, a cow, two sheep, a star in the sky, and inside under the printed "Silent Night, Holy Night" a scrawl: *Love ya, Mom.*

Snow fell every day of the week before Christmas. Ian would get off the bus in front of the barn and cross a freshly plowed road to his empty house. Just between the snowbank on the roadside and the porch steps a narrow path was stamped or shoveled by his father's big boots.

Stamped or shoveled—Ian guessed it depended on how things had gone in the barn that day.

If it wasn't shoveled, Ian did the job with the old half-handled grain shovel that kept company with an old broom on the porch. First Ian swept the porch, then he shoveled a path, not deep and even-sided like his father's work, but better than a boot-stamped one. He had figured out the order on Monday, the first day it snowed. That first day he'd made the mistake of shoveling before sweeping, and some of the white powder he sent flying off the porch landed in his path and undid his hard work.

Jeez, he'd said to himself, that was dumb. He was glad neither his father nor Ray had seen and called him dumb first.

Also on Monday, with no one looking, he'd made a snow angel in the smooth snow in front of the porch where Mom planted flowers in the summertime. He lay down, flapped his arms and legs, and got up carefully to examine his work. He was pleased with the hard pressed head, the expansive wings, the wide skirt.

But on Tuesday, as he lay in the soft, new snow covering the first angel and moved his limbs, he pictured that skirt and felt a rush of embarrassment. He used to do this with Mom, but now he was too old. What if Ray saw him? He jumped to his feet and marched all over the mold, stamping boot tracks into the angel.

Wednesday, Thursday, Friday—each day it snowed;

snow covered the path and yard. But something weird happened. Each day after school, before he swept and shoveled, he found a large angel flying in the snow by the porch.

Ian never asked who made them. He didn't want to know if someone was teasing him. Must be Ray. Mom always said to ignore teasing. Still, those angels, one card, a buzz, and the newspaper that started reappearing were all there was to Christmas.

Assignment #1: Personal News

Ian's favorite part of sixth grade so far had been when Mrs. Worth taught poetry and talked about the power of words.

That was in the fall. Starting in December, Mrs. Worth had a new approach to writing. Current Events. Each month they had to write a report about an event, the Who What When Where and Why, plus a sentence or two of Personal Commentary. "Even if you can't find it within you to actually read the newspaper, I know you listen to the radio and watch TV. Turn off *The Simpsons*," she said, "and watch the news for once."

Mrs. Worth said she expected great things from her first assignment, Personal News. "It will start you on a path of self-reflection that will connect your inner selves to the outer world," she told them.

Riding home, Ian sat by himself on the bus and thought about possible Personal News items.

First idea: *My mother left November 15.* No good. Too personal.

Second: *We have stray voltage in the barn.* Naw. He could never explain the What. Too complicated. All watts! Too much work to be funny. And it wasn't funny.

How about: *It snowed yesterday. Four inches.* No, that was dumb. So what if it snowed?

So what was left? The kitten. He was new, for early Christmas, so he was news. Get it? His mind hooked onto Little Guy, began to develop words. New kitten. For Christmas. Early. From my mother. Why? Good question. Maybe he would skip that part.

Once home, Ian avoided going directly to the barn; instead, he took two stale graham crackers from the kitchen and went to his room. He wrote:

BOY LOSES CATS

Ian Daley (that's me) has lost two yellow cats in two years at his farm in Greensbook, Vermont.

The first ones name was Golden Guernsey and he was my all time favorite because he was my first cat that I got for my fifth birthday. Then one February, poof! he didn't come in for breakfast. Not that day or the next or the next. My dad thinks it was coydogs which are very scarey when they howl down by the stream at night.

After that I got another kitten in June. It was the same color as Guernsey only not so much white on his belly, name of Pumpkin. In February this year he vanished. Only it was in the day time so that is even more mysterious. I saw him in the morning by his food dish and after school voila, no cat. Never saw him again. What I remember is he loved to slide along on his side chasing his tail. My mother laughed until she cried. And she cried when he was gone. "I can't believe it," was what she said. Now I have number three but I just call him little guy. And I don't know him too much yet. My mom gave him for early Christmas in November. He has a red coller. That is the first cat of mine to wear a coller.

I guess there is too many coydogs per cat around here.

That is the story of my personal news from Daley Farm in Greensbrook, VT.

Ian began to think his report was weird, too long, after he read his friend Keith's on the bus next morning:

PERSONAL NEWS

Friday we bete Richfield 10-1 in indoor soccer. We whipped there buts. I got 5. But I am not a ball hog. Only I play forward so I am there to score. Ask the coach.

We play Nordic Spirit U-12 next week. They mite kill us. Maybe not.

But Mrs. Worth liked Ian's just fine and gave him an A-with some spelling and other corrections. "Remember," she wrote, "G.U.M.!! Grammar. Usage. Mechanics." She also noted in the margin that "what we call coydogs are technically coyotes." She could try telling that to his dad. Or not.

If it weren't for Mrs. Worth, January would have been even worse than December.

Dad seemed scary, he was so gruff and far away, a bear in the woods. Ray still joked with him, but Dad had stopped joking back, and once he even pushed Ray into the gutter when Frieda kicked off a milker while Ray was supposed to be milking. Dad said, "If you're here to work, pay attention. If not, get out."

Ray started to mutter about the stray voltage making the cows crazy, and Dad just yelled, "Shut up!"

The stray voltage, more even than Mom leaving, was making Dad crazy. Maybe it had made Mom crazy enough to leave.

No one in Ian's family had ever been what you would call chatty. Not even Mom, although she did say "How are you" and "Good night" and stuff like that, and pretty things like "Morning, Sunshine!" After she left, it was quieter. But not like peace and quiet. Now no one talked but everything felt unsettled—especially the things he couldn't see: the electricity in the barn, Dad's mood, his own gut.

It felt like dark bubbling. Like pans of sap boiling alone

with no one drawing off syrup, or breathing the steam, no one noticing questions evaporating into the air. Maybe what was left would burn.

Ian was glad Mrs. Worth made them write things down. Unlike when he was in fifth grade, or fourth, he suddenly had things to say and nowhere but school to say them. She was helping him put things together.

Ian had liked school ever since kindergarten. Greensbrook Central looked like a gray warehouse on the outside but inside was filled with art projects and mostly smiling grownups. His worst experience had come in fifth grade when a substitute told him and Sarah Conroy, the only other farm kid in the class, to put their boots outside, they made the whole room smell like a barn. Some of the regular teachers had grown up on farms and his mother had always said they were the nicest bunch in the world. "Yeah, the mean ones died after we got done with them," Dad used to joke.

The one teacher still there from his parents' school days was Mrs. Worth. "Jeez! Thirty years in the sixth grade!" his father said when Ian started her class in September. "Must be dumb as she is ugly."

No one laughed at that joke. Not even Ray. Ian figured after just one day that Mrs. Worth wasn't dumb. Her classroom was decorated with masks and pictures, instruments, and dolls from trips around the world. On her desk was a framed aerial photo of the Timmons farm in

North Greensbrook, where she had grown up and where her brother still farmed. She had attached a caption and quoted it to the sixth graders from time to time: *Know your roots and grow from there.* Her son was a pilot and her daughter was Dr. Worth, one of the local vets. All in all, Mrs. Worth seemed to Ian like a reliable source of information.

Ian also did not think Mrs. Worth was ugly, although he wasn't exactly sure how he would describe her. She was taller even than Shirley LaRocque, who was the tallest sixth grader, and she wasn't either skinny or fat. Who knew? She wore long skirts. Her glasses had heavy black frames, not little golden wires like the ones Ms. Reis in third grade wore. Mrs. Worth's hair was short and straight black with clear white streaks that reminded Ian of a skunk, although he kept that thought to himself. She did have big hands and when she wrote on the dry-erase board Ian could see muscles moving under the skin of her arm. At those times, she actually looked to Ian like a big, strong Holstein cow, a boss cow; Ian was surprised that his father hadn't noticed it and appreciated it because he had once told Ian that the only female coming close to Mom's beauty was Ruby, his favorite cow.

Beauty or not, Mrs. Worth knew how to make kids work. Starting with poetry in September. August actually. School had started before Labor Day when it was hot. Seemed like the hottest, sunniest summer weather waited for the bus to haul off Ian and his friends before it showed up.

Ian had just been settling into a warm afternoon of snoozing, following a morning of desk arranging, book covering, and paper sorting, when Mrs. Worth began to read poems. She started with Robert Frost's "Birches," which woke him up a little, and by the time she got to "Stopping By Woods on a Snowy Evening" he was feeling cooler and alert and had even stopped coloring his—used to be Ray's—old white sneakers black with a marker.

Then Mrs. Worth told them to make a poem out of their names, each letter the start of a new line, as a way for her to get to know them. Silas volunteered to read his—goofy Silas, who always laughed and got in trouble for being too loud:

Summer
Is
Like
A
Song.

Ian felt goosebumps tickle his arms in spite of the heat. His own poem went:

I'm
An animal
Nobody knows.

He was too shy to read aloud, but he liked it and felt it fit like the new T-shirt he was wearing, which had never been Ray's. And when Mrs. Worth gave it back to him the next day with the comment "Ian, this is powerful. I love mysteries, but I hope I can get to know you quite well this year," he smiled even though he didn't exactly understand what she meant.

That was early in the fall and before Mom left. By November, they were done with poetry and had started reading *A Day No Pigs Would Die* in Language Arts. By then Ian had guessed Mrs. Worth's favorite subject must be social studies. All fall she kept adding to a big bulletin board of newspaper stories and cartoons about world happenings. They had to locate the events on a map and talk about why such things might be occurring.

For Ian it was a puzzle with too many pieces, because he rarely knew where places were. Indonesia had floods, Long Island had a plane crash—they were all the same to him. He knew Greensbrook. He knew his farm. That was it.

When Ian was a very small boy, he thought of their barn at night as a boat, the side windows bright like portholes lit in a puzzle Mom had of the *Titanic*, 1000 pieces. He bet their barn was bigger. A big one at sea in the pasture chugging along a steady route—he knew it was called Route 14. The road was liquid water and the barn a boat and he, Mom, Dad, Ray, and the cows were all on board together.

When he crossed the road to the house with his mother after chores, he pretended they'd reached an island in the sea. It was warm and smelled like toast and coffee and wood smoke.

He and his mother arrived first, but everyone made it to the island. His father last—he was the captain of the barn and could leave the girls only when he was sure they were safe for the night. Then he stayed with everyone on the island and ate and snored in the brown chair. Ian knew they didn't have to worry about pirates or other bad guys, his dad snored so loud. And he growled at strangers and, besides that, he had a gun in the woodshed cave.

Ian had been surprised to learn in third grade that Vermont didn't touch an ocean. He had always felt sure that around his land was the wide, lonely stretch of the sea.

In third grade too they had studied the solar system, and Ian was reassured. Vermont may not touch the ocean, but it does reach the sky. The bigness and isolation of his farm might come from floating in the sealike sky.

Water and air—Ms. Reis said they were related. She spoke of the elements. Some birds fly in the air and some, like the wood ducks on Jiggles Brook, fly on the water. They just have to be in their element. Ms. Reis said people were the same, they just had to find their element before they could do what they were meant to do.

He figured the farm was his element and he would stay there forever. Maybe not farming, because Dad wanted

Ray to do that, but running a business from the farm, like Aunt Julie's HAIRCARE CLASSIQUE. Or maybe he would be a vet and build a house down near their stream and drive a truck to other farms to take care of cows and have a clinic at the house for cats and dogs, although he didn't like dogs much. His parents could retire to Florida as they used to joke about doing. Other than that, he hadn't thought much about the wide world.

But in spite of social studies, he liked sixth grade and the funny way Mrs. Worth called him Master Daley. He began to wonder about other places. He began to read his mother's newspaper and he began listening when news came on the radio in the barn at milking time.

Ian woke on Groundhog Day with the sun in his eyes. Light, worse than the alarm clock he forgot to set, made him turn to his side and pull the quilt over his head. It must be late. He listened. No milk pump. A car's swoosh. Then quiet... and drip. Another drip outside his window. He rolled over, away from the warm burst of white coming in from the east, and squinted at the window. Yesterday it had been frosted opaque; today it showed patches of sky blue and icicles from the roof above melting in front of his eyes. He needed to pee.

The whoosh and crash of snow sliding off the shed roof startled him. He got up and looked out to see if anything, like maybe Little Guy, had been caught in the avalanche. A white pile glistened. No signs of life. Across the road the steep barn roof faced him, its western side still shaded and white, still piled with snow. Later it would slide. Ian imagined the sound startling him again and wondered if Dad or Ray or he himself passing to the barn would get hit by the fall. They never had. Maybe today. He felt nervous as he went down the stairs. Maybe this would be his day to be caught and buried in the sliding snow.

Downstairs, no one about. It was late. A greasy fry pan sat on the stove. Egg carton, jars, a stick of butter in its paper, plates, mugs, papers cluttered the counter. Cupboard doors swung open. The refrigerator hummed. Ian touched the woodstove tentatively. Warm, but barely. He opened its door, thinking he'd stir the ashes in a minute. First he went to the bathroom.

There he looked at himself in the mirror. Spread his lips wide, smile-like, saw dull eyes, and scowled, making his eyes squinty, mean, his lips a short, flat line. Like Dad's. *You, boy, wipe that smile away. Get to work. Hey, you. Where you been? Sleeping! You're a bum.* Yup, he could sound just like Dad.

Ian shrugged and let his eyes cross. He stuck out his tongue.

Back to the living room with its patches of sunlight. The sound of dripping water had followed him down-stairs. Too hot to stoke the fire. He swung the stove door closed and snapped the latch. Not hungry, and still in pajamas, he pulled on boots and stepped outside.

A Vermont farm. Midwinter. Snowbanks as high as a car's roof along the straight stretch of valley road.

Ian looked about him at the bright beautiful dripping thawing February day and thought, Groundhog Day, "Half your wood and half your hay," that's the saying. This winter had been too long already, and the idea of only being midway through weighted him as though he were really buried under an avalanche. Everything was a mess: the farm, his missing mother, his distant father and brother, his weird aunt. What good did he have? A sunny day, scenery like a calendar, a bunch of cows, a kitten, some friends he got to see only at school, and his teacher.

Assignment #2: Local News

Back in January Ian had left his A- on the kitchen counter with all the loose papers heaped there. The mail, the DHIA milk-testing papers, phone messages, and a shopping list with "toilet paper" in Aunt Julie's handwriting. Ian hoped she would notice it as she had his pathetic Christmas list, and show it to Dad. Dad sometimes paid attention to what Aunt Julie said. He treated her differently from how he treated Ian or Ray and definitely differently from how he had treated Mom. Dad ordered Ray around or joked with him. He ignored Ian. He had yelled at Mom or ignored her. He was never sparkly or kind like Mom. Except a tiny bit now with Aunt Julie. He treated her as if he was grateful. He kept saying, "Thanks, Julie." And "Okay, Julie," and "Uh-huh," and "Yup."

So if she were to say, "Hey, look, Warren. The boy's got an A here, on what? Current

Events. Ian, that's great," who knew what his dad would say?

If she did say that, he might nod and say, "Okay, Ian," before gulping his coffee and going back to the barn. And maybe he'd add, "That Worth can teach. Uglier than sin, but she taught me one or two things."

Unless it was one of the bad days. You never could tell. Since the start of the stray voltage problem bad days popped up like beads of sweat, like pimples on Ray's face. You wouldn't notice anything for a while, then *wham*, an ugly mess causing lots of cursing and slamming and a general bad mood. And that was even before Mom left.

The stray voltage had started with the ice storm last winter. For two days in January it rained, and with the temperature at 32°F, instead of running along as rain ought to do, or piling softly and neatly as snow does, it turned into ice, and glazed everything. Everything: roads, vehicles, trees, bushes, mailboxes, manure chutes, silos, telephone and electric power poles. Ice thick as a storm-window pane.

The whole world hung weighted and shiny, incredibly heavy. Schools closed, radios told people to stay home and off the roads. Not a car passed between the Daley house and barn for ten hours, not even the milk truck. The Daleys' bulk tank was filled to overflowing for the first time Ian had ever seen.

Ian and Ray had boot-skated on black ice across the road to the barn when they realized that school was not even a remote possibility. Mom and Dad, tight-lipped, went about chores as always, but with Ian and Ray helping. It was strange to have the whole family together in the barn on a weekday morning. Ian had even tucked Pumpkin into his coat, bringing him to the barn for the first time. Usually content in the house, the kitten had seemed scared this morning. Here in the barn he was lulled by distractions, sniffing at everything and chasing balls of sawdust that flew from Ian's shovel as he bedded the cows.

Ian, too, felt calm and safe in the barn with only the faint but steady thrumming on the metal roof high above the haymow to remind him of the storm outside. His mother was milking and assigned him the easy jobs of calf feeding, shaking out hay for the dry cows, and giving minerals to the milkers as Ray grained them.

Ian was dimly aware of his father struggling. He was glad not to be him. He didn't have to slide along the outside manure chute trying to loosen iced gutter-cleaner paddles with a crowbar. Ian heard *thud, thud, thud* over and over. He was glad not to be the one out in the rain trying to get the tractor going, trying to get the manure out of the barn and then moved to where they piled it for the winter with a tractor and dump cart sliding on the slick driveway. Ian wasn't the one slipping on the glazed fenders and scraping his knuckles, in and out of wet gloves, against frozen metal dozens of times. He wasn't wet all that day, bruised and worried-looking, like his dad.

And he didn't have to call the Co-op half a dozen times like Mom to find out when the milk truck would come. If it didn't come by afternoon, she said, they'd have to dump the evening's milk, there was no room in the tank. Ian heard her worried voice on the barn phone but couldn't quite believe there was a problem. He listened to the agitator on the big bulk tank humming to cool the morning's milk. The usual milkhouse sound. Comforting. And so much milk seemed good. Abundance. The truck must be going to come. The ice would melt. His parents always worried and then fixed the problems. It was warm in the barn and he felt safe.

For him it was a day off. And for Ray, who droned along with WOKO as he helped Mom pour the last pail into the dumping station that pumped the milk to the bulk tank. When Ray zoomed the feed cart down the manger serving silage to the cows, he yelled at Pumpkin, "Outta the way, fleabag," but his voice was friendly.

Ray even helped Ian throw down hay. Up in the big mow they slowed down, rested on bales, and listened to the rain drumming on the roof overhead.

"Mom and Dad are so quiet," Ian said, but Ray told him they were just listening for weather reports on the radio and worried about the milk getting picked up.

"And hell, they're busy," Ray added. "They want to get done. You think they just do chores all day when you're at school? Look at Dad, he's all wet, for cryin' out loud. Hasn't even had breakfast yet."

Ian was about to ask Ray just what Mom and Dad did do all day in winter if it wasn't chores, when the crashing began. Glass breaking. Must be all the windows in the barn, by the sound of it.

Ian looked up to the one glass window high at the end of the loft. Not broken.

"What the heck?" Ray beat him to the ladder and down to the stable. The rows of windows were like bright faces behind the cows, all intact, fogged and dripping.

"Mom, what broke? We heard ..." Ian went to his mother, who was standing at the open back barn door, white, shaking her head.

"I think it's the trees. They're cracking up. I never heard it like this."

Ian followed her gaze across the glassy pasture, where every blade of brown grass, every stalk of winter weed, was encased like a frozen finger pointing up from the ground. From beyond, in the woods that climbed uphill, a stand of sugar maples, birch, and poplar, he heard it again and again. Every few seconds a sharp crack, and the tinkling of hundreds of windows and glasses as branches weighted with ice gave in and crashed to the forest floor.

And then the lights flickered. The fans groaned and

revived. The radio crackled. Lights went out. Silence.

"Hey!" Ray sounded indignant, and loud.

"Whadya expect?" Dad had said. "All the trees ain't falling on each other. I bet there's miles of lines knocked down."

That sound again—the crash and the tinkle from the woods but also from all around the barn, from the road-side, across the road, down by the river, along the road far up and down their valley. The crashing was everywhere, not just what he could see. Everything was shattering.

Ian followed his mother to the milkhouse and looked out the door at Route 14. High cables should stretch above the long road, dotted with birds, supported by poles dodging among the trees. These were the wires that guided his mind's eye and pulled him forward as he rode the bus every morning and gazed sleepily out the foggy window.

Now the power lines sagged in places under the weight of half-frozen birds; they snapped here and there from the sharp edges and glassy shards of falling branches. His mother closed the door and moved to the window, frightening Ian with her wide-eyed staring.

He went back to the stable. Each sound—the rattle of a neckchain, a snort, a cough, a flap of a waterbowl paddle—hung alone and loud in the dim barn. He lingered by the calf stalls, where even the usually frisky babies stood with ears flared, listening.

Only Dad was in motion, whipping down the walk

behind the cows, out the side door, into the rain again, to the equipment shed, wrestling the generator into place against the transformer on a power pole.

Later that week, at school, other kids spoke of a few days without lights, no running water, no TV. Silas said the meat in their freezer went bad, but so did the frozen brussels sprouts and broccoli, and his mother let them eat up all the melting ice cream. Keith said the worst for him was missing *Monday Night Football*, and not taking a shower for three days.

But for the Daleys the power problems had never ended. There was no doubt in Ian's mind, even a year later, what he would write about for his Local News when he saw the headline "Stray Voltage Plagues Farms." Hey, he thought, stunned, that's us. He wrote:

STRAY VOLTAGE PLAGUES FARMS

One year ago there was the ice storm. For some farms there are still problems with the power and it is called stray voltage. It is when the electricity escapes where it should go in the wires but Springline Public Service says it's almost fixed.

The article says this is a bigger problem in the mid-west than here and that is something because I thought we were the only ones.

Well, ever since the ice storm the electricity in our barn has gone crazy. We get zapped all the time from our stall dividers and any old pipe. Last summer my brother Ray touched a milk pail to the dumping station and pretty near got electrocuted. He howled like he was stung by 3 billion bees and dropped the pail which was full of milk. That's not the only milk we've lost.

The cows get zapped from wet cement and from their water-bowls so they don't drink much. Well, would you? And since they don't drink they don't give much milk. As you probly know, milk is mostly 90% water.

Springline Public Service (SPS) has been here a lot and they put a block on the line between the pole and the barn after Ray got zapped. It worked for a week but the problems came back. We had to beef Valentine when she got mastitis from not milking out good and Mom said her heart was broken.

Then SPS said they couldn't do anything. And we must have bad management on the farm.

There are other farms on Route 14 with problems of stray voltage. But Mom said we have it the worst. Somedays Dad shuts off the power at the barn and uses the generator but that is expensive to buy diesel for it and besides the cows are used to being too scared to drink.

Electricity is no good unless it is in the right place under control.

After Ian wrote that for school, he wrote this on another piece of paper and taped it above his desk: *Electricity is a wild beast.* The words just came to him. Weird but true.

A few days later, when he got the paper back with corrections and another A-, he put it in an envelope to send to his mother. He almost added the small scrap of paper. He wanted to tell her that he knew how she felt being here with the power gone crazy, that she wasn't the only one. Thoughts swirled through his head. There was the coydog who snatched Guernsey from his hunting route. A wild beast. Just like the stray voltage sneaking into their barn picking fights, making everyone jittery, hurting the cows through their water and their floor. Shocking them through metal pipes, hiding out in the ground and leaping out at them, all of them, anytime it felt like it. A wild beast—and if the electricity didn't bother Pumpkin, a coydog got him. Okay, Mrs. Worth, a coyote. Probably would be one for Little Guy. There was something bad here for every creature.

My news, Mom, Ian thought, is like this: Wild beasts everywhere. The world in Greensbrook is unsafe. You can't live a peaceful life here. It looks okay, peaceful even, actually beautiful. It looks like the postcards in Avery's Store or on the Co-op's calendar. Hills behind farms. Easy shapes to draw, like in art class. Rectangular white barns and cylindrical silos. White house boxes with lots of windows, more boxes with crosses to show the panes of glass. Slanted roof lines. Maple trees with symmetrical opposite branching, and pine, spruce, or cedar long, tall triangles, and in the background great humps of rolling hills. In between, squares of fields. Of course, when you hay them you realize that none of them are square. The windrows you rake never come out even. But it's all nice and restful to look at on the calendar. Restful to draw. Easy. Maybe easy for God to make. Lots of land forms. No people in sight. Or animals either, in the winter scenes. They'd all be inside. Inside. Or in the woods. Underneath. Or hiding. That's where the trouble is. That's where the news comes from. Coydogs in those pretty woods. Stray voltage underground and climbing all through that pretty barn. And cows hurting, people fighting, losing money, cats disappearing, moms leaving.

Ian felt so tired. He left the envelope on his desk and lay down alone in the dark.

The hum of the generator told him Dad and Ray were still milking. He was sorry Aunt Julie hadn't stayed late to eat with them. She was better than just Dad and Ray. But why should she stay? She had her own house.

Mom, Ian whispered into the dark room. Mom, come get me. How could you leave me here? They don't want me here. I miss you. At least you noticed me. You are so mean. What if I got zapped, or eaten? I hate you. If you come back now I won't say it again.

Tears were dripping into his ears and his pillow was getting wet, but he didn't care. Why stop crying? No one could hear him anyway. He could cry or yell at her or call for her or call her name and it didn't matter. He was alone.

Ian heard scratches on the bare stairs. Little Guy.

He called softly, "Little Guy, c'mere." The kitten

didn't come. Maybe he paused at Ian's door. All Ian could hear was the scratchy rush and rolling sound of Little Guy batting a pencil or something on the wood floor of the hallway outside his door.

That was too much. Ian wouldn't put up with being ignored by his own kitten. First Mom went off to think, now her dumb little messenger would rather play with a pencil. Ian jumped out of bed, darted out to the hallway, cornered him and scooped him up. "Gotcha," Ian hissed, and he cradled the furball with more gentleness than he felt. "I won't hurt you. Never, never, never," he told the kitten and himself. Ian knew that Little Guy would never settle into bed and sleep the way he did a month ago, but struggling with the kitten and dodging scratches was better than lying there and crying in the dark by himself.

Assignment #3: State News

The next Friday Ian came home to an empty house with the usual blank, staring windows. When he got off the bus in front of the barn, the sun seemed suddenly so bright and friendly that he didn't want to go inside. The sky was shockingly blue, higher than he remembered it. He'd gone to school in frosty thin sunlight that morning and here it was 3:30, still warm, still day. Winter was beginning to end, now that days outlived school hours. Would there be anything for him here at home? He looked across the road at the lonely house and the white field sloping to the stream beyond it. The melting snow sparkled so brightly his eyes hurt. He had never before thought of leaving this farm. But it pained him now, seemed sharp as glass. Could he look somewhere else, the way Mom did?

He turned to the barn and the wooded hillside behind it. The cows were outside, milling about. Only a few had ventured off the cement pad behind the building. Those brave ones stood at the edge of the snow-frosted pasture with heads hanging, waiting maybe for the grass they recollected to appear. Gloria licked the snow, shook her big black head, snorted. She licked again. Most stood calmly as though sunbathing, eyes half closed, chewing, occasionally dropping manure.

"Hey, girls." Ian walked around to the fence. "Pretty nice out, huh?"

He figured Dad had let them out while cleaning the barn, and suddenly Ian wanted to see him. To get back to normal, minus the sharp, energizing sun. He just wanted to say "Hey, Dad" and hear his reliable grunt.

But the barn was empty, and the gutters were clean, the stalls bedded with fresh sawdust. No Dad. Ian stood by the back door watching the cows—out, unattended. Just them, and him, in the sun.

Then he heard the sputter and whine of a chainsaw. A revving and a sputtering. Again. The thump of log against log, way up on the hill. Oh, yeah. Dad was in the woods, clearing up. That morning he'd said it was time to get going on sugaring. Those trees they didn't tap last year because of the ice storm—their vacation was over. "Ray," Dad had said, "if there's light when you get home, start chores, 'cause I'll be in the woods." Ray must be up there too. He'd done his work in the barn. Good old Ray, always on the ball.

Ian felt left out of their efficient work program. He had been Mom's helper; Ray was Dad's. Now what was left? Old cruddy crackers, homework, TV. He crossed to the house side of the road, pulled the newspaper from its tube, and trudged inside.

In the house, Ian surprised himself. He didn't want to eat or watch TV. State News was due, but any news seemed boring when the sun was alive and his dad was moving trees in the woods. He almost wanted to go up there and help. But not exactly. He was afraid of not knowing what to do. He was afraid of getting in Dad's way.

If his mother were here, he thought for the millionth time, there would be no problem. He needed her in between. She was his pillow against Dad's rough voice and way of giving directions. "Hold it," his dad would say, talking more to the log than to him, and his mother would show him just where to place his hands, how to push and then ease up.

Forget it, he said to himself with a sigh. Might as well do what he knew how to do. Get another friggin' A-. Ian spread out the newspaper on the kitchen counter. The legislature blah blah. Governor Dean blah blah. Maybe he'd better have a snack. Ian opened the refrigerator.

Gross. Aunt Julie was right. He started pulling out mayonnaise and pickle jars, catsup and lemon juice bottles. Here was something he could do.

Soon the entire editorial, commentary, and letters-to-the-editor section was covered with containers: plastic catsup, mustard, salad dressing bottles, the metal milk jug, a sticky carton of orange juice that was almost empty, old hot dogs in a dripping plastic bag, dry lumps of cheese, a cardboard twelve-pack of Old Milwaukee with three cans left, four quart-sized canning jars containing pickle juice (one of them might be maple syrup), and two half-pint jars of moldy jam. That was from the shelves. He still had the inside of the door and the crisper drawers to go. And the freezer, he thought, but maybe he'd leave that for another time.

The other day Aunt Julie said she couldn't find anything in here. Then she said "Ugh" and "Yuck" as she unfolded foil packets and smelled jars. "Oh my God," she said, "I never seen sauerkraut this color." It was purplish gray. "Mariette hasn't made sauerkraut in years. Ian, this must be old as you!"

No wonder nobody ate it, Ian thought. But Aunt Julie wasn't done. "Don't you guys ever clean this out? Ray, you could do this, you know. Your mother couldn't do everything. The house. The barn. The bills. Two lazy boys."

"Chill," Ray said, "like a refrigerator."

Aunt Julie was fuming mad. She slapped old cheese on the counter. How could his mother's twin have a temper so like his father's? Ian didn't get it.

"It's unhealthy," she said, "your milkroom, spotless, and your kitchen, a pigsty. I hate farming."

How could she hate farming when she lived on a farm and visited theirs so often? And why did some moldy food in a refrigerator make her cry? He knew she'd been married once, but he didn't remember Uncle Fred. He was a drinker, Aunt Julie said, a funny guy but a drinker nonetheless. She liked a joke as much as the next guy, she said, but she did not like a drunk. Ray once told Ian that all he remembered about Uncle Fred was him rolling bread into tiny balls one Thanksgiving and tossing them across the table over the turkey.

Once the food was out of the refrigerator, Ian could see that the shelves were kind of grungy and sticky with globs of catsup, maybe, and something like white crust. He filled the sink with hot water, squirted in some dish soap, and set to work with a sponge cleaning the shelves, walls, drawers, and compartments of the refrigerator. Simple. Then he put everything back neatly, throwing away the dried-out cheese, the stinky hot dogs, and the jam jars. Too bad to waste the glass jars—his mother would never do that—but he was too tired to wash them. He also threw out some pickled beets, which he hated. He smiled. Mom and Dad loved pickled beets, yup, they had that in common, but they weren't doing this job, were they? Besides, the jar looked old, with faded writing on the handwritten label. Maybe he was saving their lives by tossing the beets. Dad's life, anyway. Hadn't he heard Mrs. Worth mention canned goods and botulism in the same breath? Another reason to toss the jars.

Ian was pleased with his work. But he felt bad leaving the door open for so long. He knew he was wasting electricity. Could you turn the refrigerator off? Maybe he should have unplugged it while he worked, but the plug was way around back and the thing bulky. Besides, plugging and unplugging scared him.

Then he noticed the newspaper on the counter, spotted now with red drips and blotches of soapy water. For his State News he picked one of the few dry articles, a short one in the far-right column. He read it and then wrote:

DRUNKEN DRIVING BILL
LOSES MOMENTUM

Governor Howard Dean has plans to stop drunken drivers. If a drunk driver is caught by the police he or she will have a "scarlet letter" decal put on their license plate. This law goes with the original laws like fines for drunk drivers. The law might not be voted for this year because the State House has been working on something else and Dean hasn't helped them.

An opinion, a personal comment? Ian added, *I hope it passes,* and stuffed the sheet of paper in his backpack for tomorrow. Short, but at least it was done. Today, he had other things than homework on his mind.

Ian went to the living room window and looked across the road and toward the hillside, wishing he had gone to work with his father up in the woods. No, wishing everything were different. He wished he could automatically know he would be welcome in the woods. He wished there were a note on the counter. Ian scribbled what it would say on an old breeding slip on his mom's desk by the window: *Hey Ian, grab some grub and meet me in the woods. Follow the buzz, love, Dad.*

Ian smiled because his dad would never in a million years write something like that. Or would he? It did sort of sound like what he'd write if he wrote notes. If it would even occur to him to write to his kid. Could he even write? Yeah, sure, there by the phone on the pile of papers was Dad's scrawl. Looked like: *Tues 8:30 vet.* He could write all right. So why did only Mom write notes? She did them all the time. Notes to his teacher, to Ray, supply shopping lists, food shopping lists, cows-to-check lists, chore lists, "To Do" lists, all kinds of lists, and phone messages: *Keith called. Silas called. Ray, call Pat. Ian and Ray dentist 8:30 Tues.* And then there were Mom's notes to him, Ian, personal notes. Ian turned his father's scrap over and wrote:

Ian, welcome home.
Find us in the sugar woods.

I'll watch for you.
Mom

Always set up like this. When Mrs. Worth taught them poetry last term, he'd thought of it then, that Mom's notes always looked like poems. Ian pulled out another scrap of paper and wrote a new name poem for himself:

Invisible parents
Argue all
Night.

And one for Mom:

Must
Of been
Miserable.

The house cast a shadow between Ian and the barn across the road. He could still hear the occasional whine of the chainsaw through the closed window, but he knew Ray had to be down from the woods by now because the lights in the barn were on. He wished his brother would come say hi. He ought to go help get the cows in.

Ian looked around the dim room, at the food-splotched newspaper covering the kitchen counter, and it came to him suddenly: Me too. Just like Aunt Julie. I hate farming. Why do I have to stay here when Mom can leave and Aunt Julie can go home? Forget it. He quickly dumped his books on the sofa and ran up the stairs to get a warm shirt and some socks. He grabbed the envelope addressed to his mother from his desk, deciding as he ran that he would deliver it to her in Barre himself. I'll ask her if I can stay at Uncle Jack's too, he thought suddenly. I can go to school there, and why not? Why do I have to stay here?

He began to breathe fast, deeply, and to smile. He'd figured out what to do. It made perfect sense.

True, he wouldn't have more than a couple of hours of light for his walk to Barre, and he wasn't sure how long it would take. But he could walk in the dark. Couldn't get lost. Just follow the road.

Little Guy tried to follow Ian out to the porch. Ian shooed him back inside and quickly shut the door. This was no trip for a cat. If he had a dog he'd take him. A dog seemed more the traveling type.

He crossed the road to the barn side. The cows were still out, and the chainsaw still whined. He headed north. Straight north, that much he knew. They used to drive to Johnson's Market there every week. Now just Aunt Julie shopped for them; he hadn't been out of Greensbrook all winter. Some of the cows walked along with him, hugging their side of the fence that edged the road. I should bring you girls too, he thought. I'm not leaving because of you. He looked back at his house then, and at the field across the road, sloping down to his swimming spot in the stream. Or any of you, he added. "Sorry, but you wouldn't like Barre," he told the cows.

He waved at Aunt Julie's mailbox and sign as he passed them and blew a kiss that Aunt Julie would never see in the direction of the home farm, way at the end of the long driveway. Whoa, he thought, that's weird. But nobody saw; he was alone on the road. Besides, Aunt Julie was all right. She had been trying, he knew, to be nice, and he also knew that it didn't come easy to her. Well, she'd guess where he was in case anyone was wondering. She was the one who gave him Uncle Jack's address in the first place. *Go ahead,* she said, *write if you want. Your mother's just trying to figure out some things.*

By now Ian had gone a mile and was halfway to the center of North Greensbook, walking steadily, but his feet were getting cold. Only a few cars and several trucks had zoomed by him. After the first car, he remembered from a SkillBuilder that he ought to be walking facing the traffic, so he crossed the blacktop again and for a minute began to feel silly. Was this a game or was it possible that he was really walking to Barre? Should he stop and put on his spare socks or wait until his feet actually hurt?

He was passing the Stanley farm now. A mixer wagon spewed feed into an outdoor bunk and big heifers were jostling each other for a better position. The Stanleys fed more corn than his dad did, and the smell was sweeter, stronger. Those heifers were bigger than Dad's.

Ian hurried along. He didn't think anyone would notice him really. Everyone pretty much kept to themselves on this road unless you asked for help, and then they'd be nice the way Dad was when Mr. Stanley hurt his back and all the men helped do his second cut.

But just in case anyone noticed him and asked, Ian thought about what he could say he was doing. He couldn't tell the truth. It would seem dumb. Why would he be going to his mother all the way to Barre, and so close to chore time? Like he was taking sides against his dad. Everyone must think he belonged here in Greensbrook, or wouldn't someone have taken him to Mom before now? Nah, he was going to Uncle Norman's in Williamstown for a magnet. Not too far away. Uncle Norman was his dad's uncle; they didn't really talk much, but they did lend things back and forth from time to time.

And why was he walking? Well, neither truck would start. That wouldn't surprise anybody. And besides, Dad and Ray had to finish in the woods and Dad left him a message to get the magnet for Lucy before chores.

Ian was thinking so hard about his alibi that he was surprised to see Avery's just ahead. He realized he had forgotten to bring any money and that what was now a little hunger in his gut would certainly grow. The store reminded him of food, especially of candy, which he had had mighty little of since Mom left. It didn't seem to occur to anybody to take him along for a treat now and then. If it weren't for Mrs. Worth's bribery tactics, Ian thought, he would be starving for sugar like that kid Charlie before he made it to the chocolate factory.

But now as he passed the gas pump and looked toward the store window papered over with town notices and familiar advertisements—"Cashews $2.99!" "Shoes and shirts must be worn!"—Ian felt hungry all over. He wished he could go in and pick out a Powerade or some Reese's and wait for Mom to stop gabbing to Lindy, then get in the car and go home. He even missed the car, an old blue Escort. Not that he could drive, and Ray and Dad seemed satisfied with their trucks, when they ran. But what did Mom need the car for anyway, if she was just "figuring out some things"?

His feet felt like bricks and his head and stomach ached. Maybe from the gas pumps. The smell of gasoline always gave him a headache. Ray loved it, which was yet another difference between them.

There was the sign: WILLIAMSTOWN 2, BARRE 13.

It was still light, but Ian could feel the sun losing power as it started to drop behind the hills to the west. Maybe he could really go to Uncle Norman's and get a ride from him the rest of the way.

But he couldn't ask him that. A magnet for a sick cow or the loan of a post-hole digger was one thing; a ride to an address where he wasn't even invited was another. The most he knew about Uncle Jack was that he was born "Jacques." They never visited and Dad called him Jack the Jerk. Way back in December when Ian had suggested to Ray that they go see Mom, Ray said they weren't invited. Did Uncle Norman even know about Mom? All these relatives and no one to ask for help.

He thought of Silas and Keith. They would help him if they could, but they lived clear over in West Greensbrook and he was sort of scared of their mothers. They were so into helping at school and with teams; they always asked questions and wanted to talk.

Ian decided to try hitching and had to cross back to the other side of the road again. Crossing this road was sure a big part of his days. Back and forth, house to barn and back again. Dad had told him that years ago Route 14 was a quiet dirt road and his grandfather considered it a real advantage to farm near it so you could cart milk cans easily to the creamery in South Greensbrook. That was before the granite industry up north wanted paved roads for their trucks. It was still easy for the big tankers to pick up the Daley's milk, but the road created a noisy divide between house and barn. "So dangerous," Mom said, "for people. You just have sleepy dust in your eyes some morning, and *whump,* that's the end." She crossed holding on to Ray and Ian for years; then she watched them when they crossed alone. Just this year, she had stopped even telling Ian to be careful. She was always busy tending sick cows, trying to keep them from feeling the stray voltage, paying bills. Then the last straw, in the summer, when Ray touched that milk pail to the dump station and got such a shock that he was thrown to the ground and had to go to the emergency room. Ian heard her through the hole in his floor telling Dad late that night, "He could have gotten killed. I used to think it was only the road, but this whole place is jinxed. Can't we just move?"

Ian turned around to face the oncoming cars and walked backwards. Feeling silly, he stuck out his thumb the way he'd seen Ray do once or twice before he got his license. Mom said she didn't like it, but she let him. Hey, this wasn't so hard.

Daylight was fading fast. Purple and gold showed from behind West Hill. Ian felt better when he looked at the sky. Maybe he could fool his feet and his stomach into not hurting if he looked up and away from his body. He walked backwards for a few minutes, face lifted, thumb shyly out.

A van stopped. Startled, Ian wasn't sure what to do. He couldn't see the driver for the setting sun glaring off the windshield. The headlights were on. Caught like a deer, he thought. The driver's door opened, and Ann Benoit, Keith's mother, stepped out.

"Ian, where are you going? It's getting dark."

"Oh. It's okay, I just have to get something. A magnet for my dad."

"A magnet?" Mrs. Benoit stood grinning at Ian as if she didn't get the joke but was willing to believe it was the funniest thing in the world. "Well, get in." She waved him toward the van. "So where do you need to go?"

Ian opened the passenger door and saw there was no one else inside. There was no way he could let Keith's mother help him. All those questions she'd ask. He held the open door between them as he spoke.

"It's for a sick cow, she's got hardware." Mrs. Benoit raised her eyebrows: another question. "It's when they swallow something and you give 'em a magnet and it holds the metal so they don't get cut inside." Ian doubted he was explaining even this very well. "But I can get one just up at Coutures'." He gestured toward the farm fifty yards up the road. "I don't really need a ride." Mrs. Benoit started to say something. "But thanks anyway," Ian said, closing the door, and he nodded when she said, "Are you sure?"

She got into her van and drove at a crawl ahead of him, so he waved at her and began to cut across a meadow toward the Coutures' barn lights until the van was out of sight. Then he went back to the roadside. He wiggled his numb toes inside his wet sneakers. What now? He could tell from the Coutures' lights that it was choretime, and suddenly it seemed wrong to be even this far from home. He had only gone, what? Maybe two miles. How could he ever get all the way to Barre? And even then, how would he find Uncle Jack's in the dark? He was cold and hungry and it wasn't his job to find Mom anyway. He'd rather feed the calves, help milk.

He stamped across the road one last time and decisively put out his thumb; he climbed into the first pickup that stopped. The driver was a grain salesman who knew the Daley farm sure enough and stopped a few minutes later right next to his red mailbox. Ian slid off the seat and thanked the man, who said, "Anytime." Ian's own barn lights were lit and the milk pump was on, but before he crossed the road yet again to join his father and brother, he reached into his backpack for the envelope addressed to Mrs. Mariette Daley, slipped it into the mailbox, and put up the flag.

Assignment #4: Regional News

Just before Valentine's Day the cows began to get really sick. Not just the jumpiness and low milk production they'd suffered for a year, but sick. They had the runs. Bad. Winter dysentery, the vet called it, and Ian, for the first time in his eleven years, gagged at the smell of the barn.

Once, in kindergarten, his class had come for a tour of their farm and some of the kids held their noses as Mom explained the milking equipment and the parts of a cow. She used her favorite cow, patient Luna, for a model. She let everyone try to hand-milk a squirt or two. When Luna hunched her back to pee the kids screeched and giggled.

Ian remembered his mother catching his eye, smiling and shrugging. He had been confused. What was funny? Not Luna peeing. Cows pee and poop all the time. When Keith peed on the ant hill in the school playground for target practice, *that* was funny.

Since then Ian had realized farm people were different. Not many kids lived on farms. He knew stuff they didn't. Even when he seemed to know less than they did, like about CDs, clothes, dances, even sports, he'd drawn comfort from his private stash of useful information from home, like how to use a magnet in a cow. But now he was beginning to wonder what good it did him.

This winter stink was sour and strong. Behind or under most cows was a dark pool of liquid manure Ian had to hoe into the gutter. He would just barely be done scraping and bedding the cows with extra sawdust when the pools would reappear and he'd have to do it again. When they weren't hunching painfully, the cows stood listless, most not chewing. Their eyes looked like the windows of his house when he got off the bus in the afternoon—glassy, staring, nobody home.

Two calves died on one day, Pauline's and Fancy's, sweet little heifers from two of their best cows. That night, as Ian tried to write his Regional News, he heard Dad and Aunt Julie talking downstairs. "That's a blow," his dad said. Just that—"That's a blow," Dad's gruff voice rising up through the hole in his floor—scared Ian. All along, ever since the ice storm, throughout the past year of troubles, with even Mom leaving, his dad stayed glum-faced, grouchy, or downright angry. But he never sounded touched by any of it, like in his gut. He never seemed to take it personally or let anyone know if he did. Now

"That's a blow" to Aunt Julie. His dad sounded, and this was the new thing, sad. That night Ian also heard him tell Aunt Julie, "I don't think I can hang on til spring."

By the next week two more calves had died and seven cows were dry. Milk production was so low that Dad said it hardly paid to turn on the milk pump or run the bulk tank. The big tank hummed and the agitator turned slowly, but milk was a small white puddle deep down at the bottom compared to the usual brimming load. Like the stream shrinking with the drought last summer.

Ian thought of other nights he'd listened through the old stovepipe hole in his floor. When he was little, it was comforting to hear his parents' voices drift up as he went to sleep. Then it became annoying to hear Ray down there with them when he had to be in bed. But the worst was last summer when every night brought his parents' fighting voices into his ears. Over the hole he had placed an old baby quilt, the one his mother must have removed and tucked around Little Guy the day she left him at Ian's bedside.

Ian finally found an article that would do, and wrote:

WINTERS WARMER, DRIER WEATHER
WATCHERS SAY

Are winters in Vermont getting warmer? Well, that's what Gilman Ford says. He is part of the Burlington weather watcher service.

The National weather watcher of Burlington says that years ago it was common for the temperature to be 40°F below, but now on a rare day in the winter it is 30° below.

There are 75 weather watchers in the Burlington weather watcher service.

There are 11,000 weather watchers in all 50 states and Puerto Rico and the U.S. Virgin Islands. 98% of the National weather watcher service's weather watchers come from volunteers. It's a good thing they have enough weather watchers because I think it would be too boring to be a weather watcher.

All that measuring and writing down temperatures and snowfall amount on charts, thought Ian, but he didn't add it to his paper because it was long enough. Jeez! His dad would never do that job, but his mother probably could. Just like adults, thought Ian, to ruin a perfectly simple and easy thing like watching the weather. Couldn't it be a job to just look at something and not have to take notes and make a paper of it? It wasn't that Ian was against writing. He wasn't lazy. Maybe it was the measuring part. Seemed to him enough, if his dad said, "Winters were colder when I was a kid, more snow back then too." That should be enough without having to put down numbers.

His dad did say that. Ian liked his dad's words. They gave him a picture of a bigger world, richer, tougher, and it made him see his dad the way he was on the day of the ice storm, brave, enduring hardship.

But his mom said, "You just say those things to make the boys feel small. Winter's winter. Always cold, with snow."

On Ian's paper Mrs. Worth wrote, "Is this regional or state news?" But she gave him a B+. He didn't care; it was getting harder to pay attention.

At lunchtime Keith was telling their table how he did every Current Events assignment on sports. His indoor soccer team (Personal), the high school and Ray's basketball team (Local), the new U.V.M. goalie (State), the Green Bay Packers at the Super Bowl (National), which he mixed up with Regional.

"She doesn't care," he told Ian with his mouth full. "She goes, 'You, Master Benoit, are a sports maniac. I want to see that passion in your articles every week. Only, please, combine your passion with the commonly accepted rules of spelling and G.U.M.'" He laughed out loud, spraying droplets of milk on Ian.

"Oh, Keith, Nicki has a passion for hot dogs. Don't you?" Sarah and other sixth-grade girls at the other end of the table dissolved into giggles at their joke. Keith scooped up the Tater Tots from his tray and threw several at them.

Ian looked at the little brown rolls on his own tray. And his hot dog. He wasn't hungry. Food at school never tasted the way it should. This used to be one of his favorite meals at home. His mother told him he called those potatoes "round bales" when he was little, and everyone in his house still called them that. Now they looked disgusting.

"Isn't she?" Keith was talking.

"Huh?" Ian said.

"Using the *P* word all the time, you idiot. *Passion.* Do you even know what it means?"

"What what means?" Ian wasn't hungry but wished he were.

"God, Ian! It's what Ray and what's-her-face did last year in the back of the bus. Smoochy-woochy. Somebody should tell Mrs. Worth it's nothing to do with sports, or stupid current events."

Keith started putting Ian's round bales in his mouth, one after another, until all ten loaded his cheeks like a chipmunk's. He chewed, tapped Silas on the shoulder, and opened his mouth, showing white and spit-covered gobs.

"Cool," Silas said.

In fourth grade, at Keith's urging, Ian had signed up for soccer. Not the fancy winter kind that Keith and some of the others played at an indoor sports center in Northhaven, just regular outdoor Saturday soccer sponsored by the Greensbrook recreation committee at the town ballfield. For Ian it was a big deal. For his family it was a big deal.

His father said school was enough off-farm activity for anyone, since it involved evening assemblies, conferences with teachers, and field trips as well as the regular everyday hours in the classroom. High school basketball and baseball teams for Ray, well, that was okay. An extension of school. No extra fees, uniforms, expecting parents to drive kids all over the goddamn place. In spite of his feelings Dad told both boys to do Little League if they wanted. He said he remembered wanting to and not being allowed by his father, who made his only son help on the farm all the time. "Cows don't take time off, neither can we," Dad always told Ray and Ian. "But I won't ever hold you guys hostage like my father did to me. You want to farm, fine. You want to go off and do your own thing, go."

That didn't mean he would help them go do their own thing, or drive them there, or watch games, or pay for it. Neither did he seem to want Mom doing those things. He laughed and said, "Your mother is a willing hostage."

Ray was good at baseball. He progressed from T-ball to minors to majors, then quit when the coaches wanted him for all-stars or Babe Ruth. Too many practices, too intense, Ray said. He preferred pounding posts with Dad. That was just about the time Dad let him drive the tractor. But Ray was good enough to make the high school team anyway. Dad said, "Course you are, farm work is good training for anything."

Ian couldn't see how driving a tractor would help anyone's pitching or base-running skills. He figured Ray was just one of those guys who were good at sports. Like Keith. He himself had hated minors and never made it beyond. He'd seen his mother at games talking to other parents, arranging to get him a ride home, or just sitting on the sideline of the field with her eyes half closed, chin lifted to the setting June sun, and he knew she was patiently waiting for him, waiting to take him home so she could get back to the barn and finish chores. She never said she minded. Only once, he heard a tiny sigh and saw her glance at her watch after a game that lasted past 8 p.m. Ian liked being with Keith and the other kids, he liked the coach, Silas's father, and he loved swinging the bat, even at the wild pitches of other eight-year-olds, but he hated dropping the ball or not catching it in the first place. After a while it seemed more comfortable at home.

Last fall, soccer was different. Since stray voltage had come to visit, home wasn't all that comfortable, and it was getting harder not to participate in anything else. Keith urged Ian to join, saying, "You never do anything. If I didn't know how you beat everyone in arm wrestling, I'd think you were a wimp." Kevin whacked him in the arm. "Arm like a hammer. Besides, soccer's fun. Have some fun for a change."

That first Saturday, Mom was still in the barn at 8:55, so Ray drove Ian to the rec field for the 9 a.m. practice. He pulled his truck alongside the Binghams' mini-van, or maybe it was the Coutures' identical one.

"I might need money," Ian told Ray without moving to open the door.

"Like how much? I only got a couple of bucks. Whyn't you ask Mom?" Ray began to dig in his pockets.

"I don't know," Ian said.

"Find out. Ask 'em." Was it Ian's imagination or did Ray add "you moron"? He began to wish he'd stayed home. He hated this stuff. How did anyone find out these things? Their parents found out, that was how. Why was his business always up to him? Why couldn't he just play like the other kids and leave the details to Mom or Dad (fat chance) or even Ray?

He looked at Ray's familiar face, round and strong like Mom's, not too many pimples that day, clear blue eyes already focused on someplace else, one hand tapping lightly on the steering wheel, the other holding a small fan of wrinkled dollar bills. Ray wanted to help; hadn't he driven him even though Saturday was his only day to sleep in?

But Ray was not the moms and dads starting to unload around them, shutting doors carefully, calling warnings to running children, carrying water bottles and dufflebags, purses. Those parents all looked like they owned the rec field already. It didn't seem up to him or Ray to mess with details.

"Ian, you going down or what? I gotta take off."

Ian didn't know what to do. He was about to say he guessed he'd go home.

"Hey, hurry up!" Keith's face appeared at his window, squished and pink lips pressing on the glass. His mother was smiling behind him, waving at Ray. She pulled open the door and said to Ray as Ian scrambled out, "I'll bring him home. Glad he could come."

All was well. The sky blue. The cloud gone. Keith's mother would do. He waved to Ray. You can go now. Finally someone doing her job.

That night at supper Ray said, "Ian, guess you're glad Ann Benoit saved your skin. You were too chicken to walk down there alone. Mom, you shoulda gone. It's a parent thing. You know, forms to sign, money to fork over."

"Sorry." She shrugged.

"It's okay. You didn't have to be there. I got a paper for you to sign," Ian said. Why, he wondered, did Ray always do that: do something nice like driving him this morning, and then take it back by making it seem like he was a baby and Mom was to blame.

"My father always said you can do sports or you can farm, not both," Dad said.

His father's amazing hands moved about the table feeding himself. Huge knuckles, nails dark, thick fingers, palms creased with deep black lines, maps of exploration of rough, dirty places. Maybe history people like Ethan Allen had hands like those, maybe Paul Bunyan. Not his coach, not the fathers of his friends. Even when Dad acted like a jerk, Ian was in awe of his hands and what they accomplished in a day.

Once, in second grade, they held a medieval feast and parents were invited to come in costume to eat stew and hardboiled eggs on trenchers of bread. Ian sat uneasily at the head table because Mrs. Gardner had appointed him king as a reward for getting all 100s on his spelling tests. The queen was Emily Fitzpatrick, the only other kid to get all 100s. Her father, a carpenter, had come and sat near them smiling quietly. Earlier that day Emily had announced to the class with pride, "My dad is coming 'cause he can't work 'cause yesterday he cut off his pointer finger with a saw."

Ian couldn't keep his eyes on his own trencher and goblet, nor on Keith, the jester, who was at center court juggling scarves. Ian kept looking sideways at Mr. Fitzpatrick, at the hand he ate with calmly, at the huge bandaged mitt that appeared every so often to steady a dish, adjust a cup, and then returned to his lap like a shy kid.

Ian thought of his dad's fingers. Too tough to cut off. He felt sorry for Emily's dad and ordinary digits. Everyone at their feast, including himself, seemed weak compared to his father. If only they knew that Ian was the son of a sort of king. When Mrs. Gardner addressed him as Your Majesty and begged permission for the gathering to commence recess, Ian thought maybe she did know. "Let the feast end and recess begin!" he said, louder than usual.

If his father seemed different from other parents, so

did his mother. Not that she looked too strange. Long brown hair pulled back into a ponytail. She had a round moon face and big eyes, blue eyes. When she'd been outside or working hard in the barn, dots of red glowed on each cheek and made her look happy and pretty. Her hands were callused but normal size. He used to like to trace the soft rubbery blue veins flowing through her long hand bones and knuckles. Soft but strong, like the milkhoses in the barn. Rivers of blood under control in his mother's hands. Blood, like milk, meant life.

It was his mother's liveliness, her energy, that was different, even from her twin sister. If the others were babbling brooks, she was a river. They were calm ponds, she was a wave or what he imagined a wave to be, powerful. The other mothers stood on the sidelines and watched and talked. She had bigger things to get to. He wanted to be around her, to be warmed by her, to have her point things out.

She reminded him of the woodstove at the center of their kitchen. Glowing, bright and warm, even roaring sometimes like a box of bees on a good day.

Yet all winter it was Dad who kept the woodstove going, never asked for help. Every morning. Every night. It was always going when Ian came home from school. Why had he never realized how amazing that was? Both that its warmth and fire was like Mom and that Dad always took care of it.

Ian snapped awake. A terrible dream. His cat Guernsey in a deep hole down near the stream. The hole was filling up with milk and Guernsey was licking it. Coydogs were yipping and snarling all around the top of the hole. Guernsey didn't see them, but his dad was there with a gun yelling, "Who left the damn tank open?" One dog jumped on Guernsey.

Ian lay shaken. Why didn't his dad shoot? Just a dream, but the voices ripped his ears, the yipping and his father's yells. No sense to it—they always checked the valve on the tank to make sure it was closed. He knew Guernsey would die. He couldn't stand that it would hurt. His throat felt raw as if he'd been shouting or running hard.

He lay still for several minutes; his breath came easier. He remembered it was Valentine's Day and wished he could go back to sleep and not dream.

In school, Ian felt tired; Silas asked him if he was sick and gave him his last stick of Big Red.

At recess, Mrs. Worth stopped him on his way to the playground and asked if he would like to help her set up the operating room. He shrugged and said okay, but really he was relieved not to have to run around outside when he didn't feel like it. He was, after all, one of the few who raised his hand when she asked who would be interested in examining a real heart for Valentine's Day, a calf heart from her daughter's veterinary practice. From a patient that hadn't made it. Jeez, Ian had thought, I coulda brought in lots of dead cow parts.

"Cover the table with this, please, Master Daley," she said, handing him a big plastic tablecloth covered with Winnie-the-Poohs and balloons. "This will give the squeamish ones something else to look at."

Ian tried to smile as he remembered being curious at the prospect of seeing a heart bigger than a chicken's, which was small and disappointingly like a lump of brown clay. But with all the confusion at home, he'd forgotten about it. He'd even forgotten to bring in the slip signed by a parent preapproving this unusual-for-sixth-grade science lesson. The last time she dissected something, Mrs. Worth said, she and the principal got a slew of complaints saying the kids were too young.

"One of these on each desk, please." Mrs. Worth handed him a sheaf of papers showing a diagram of a four-chambered heart with vessels and chambers labeled. "Then come look through these"—she patted a pile of permission slips in one corner of her desk—"and see if you can find yours."

Ian walked along rows of crowded desks, stepping over backpacks and sneakers, distributing the maps of the hearts. Sheepishly, he even picked at some of the notes on her desk before he said, "I forgot mine."

"Rats," Mrs. Worth said. "I was afraid of that, but I

thought it might be stuck to Keith's or Silas's with gum or some such substance."

Ian smiled, looking hopelessly at Mrs. Worth's desk.

"So, what should we do here? Have you sit out with Miss Bouvier and Miss Phelps, who persuaded their mothers not to sign the form?"

Yes, this day could so get worse, thought Ian.

"Or we could call your house and get permission by phone." Mrs. Worth looked at him over her glasses seriously as though this were a big decision.

"My mom's not there," Ian said, barely audible.

"I know, but your dad would be in for lunch, wouldn't he? Or we could try your aunt. I'm sure your parents wouldn't mind. Your mother loved science, as I recall, and your dad liked anything involving blood and guts. This is just a formality." She reached for the phone hidden under reading folders on a side cabinet. "Do you want to call or shall I?"

"You," said Ian, after hesitating. This might not be a good idea. The thought of nice Mrs. Worth brushing up against his father's gruffness worried him. But he wasn't going to call and he couldn't quite say, *Forget the heart, who cares?* So he gave his phone number and thought that with any luck Aunt Julie would still be around helping with morning chores. At least she might sound polite.

Mrs. Worth was talking into the phone and laughing. She hung up and looked at Ian.

"He says by all means, watch the heart, and if it looks okay, well, could you bring it home for supper?"

The other kids were returning from recess and she bent close to Ian to say, "Things will get better, you'll see. You are doing just the right thing. Stay busy, do your schoolwork, your chores, clown around with those two meatheads over there"—she motioned to Keith and Silas pushing each other at the water fountain—"and give your father a chance. Show him your papers and permission slips. Years ago I made sure he could sign his name."

After their talk, the sharp scent of formaldehyde, the deep cuts with the scalpel, and the clear distinction between blood vessels and the purple meat of the atrium and ventricles seemed clean and refreshing in their simplicity. After all, the calf was dead and the heart was numb. His own heart pounded and with each breath he felt a small pain.

Assignment #5: National News

It was an afternoon in March. Ian sat in his room at his desk, distracted. The sudden melt and light of February had settled into a pattern of bright, warm days and cold, frosty nights. Perfect sugaring weather. Dad spent every afternoon in the woods, grouchy that he wasn't finished tapping yet and might miss a run of sap. Ray seemed to be in charge of the barn. Most of the cows had recovered, but they remained thin and listless as though they guessed that their best days at the Daley farm might be over. Aunt Julie, now for some reason playing the role of optimist, said those poor cows were just waiting for green grass, that they, like everyone else, were sick of the damn winter.

It was awful brown outside. Mud everywhere, soupy by day, frozen at night, all the time moving from one state of matter to the other. Ian thought it was worse than piles of snow, stickier and harder to walk in. Mrs.

Worth had said that sidewalks were civilization's answer to the quagmire of mud season, and that much as she treasured her farm-girl background, she did love the sidewalks of Barre. That was where she lived now.

Quagmire. Ian said the word to himself, feeling its ugliness pulling him down.

Little Guy jumped just then onto Ian's lap, treaded in a half circle, and lay down, purring. Snaps of static buzzed Ian's hand as he stroked the black fur. He tried to concentrate on the newspaper spread out in front of him.

There was an article about the comet Hale-Bopp, but he couldn't use that. It would be bigger than National News. Mrs. Worth had said to start looking for the comet in the northwestern sky around two a.m. Wake up the whole family, she'd said.

Right. Ian could just imagine: *Dad! Ray! Let's go out at two a.m. and look at the stars!* Or a comet, or whatever. It would be like trying to wake up rocks. Now, Mom—she would like it, just her cup of tea.

He found an article that would do, read it, and wrote his own:

UNITED STATES DEPARTMENT OF AGRICULTURE (OR USDA) LEADS EFFORTS TO RESCUE FOOD FROM GARBAGE

In the United States every year people waste about 13.8 billion pounds of food. The wasted food mostly comes from hotels restaurants and grocery stores.

The U.S.D.A. has saved 150 pounds of food each week from their cafeteria in Washington, D.C.

Clinton has signed the Good Samaritan Donation Act which protects stores like 7-Eleven and Pizza Hut from having to pay if they donate food and the person got sick who ate it.

The nation's biggest distributor of perishable recovered food, the Food Chain of Kansas City, Mo., collected more than 100 million pounds of food last year in 42 states.

I hope that next year there won't be 13.8 billion pounds of food wasted.

It was getting too easy to write these stupid articles. Maybe he should send another of his assignments to Mom so she could see how stupid life was. But he hadn't heard from her at all since her dumb card. It was her turn to write. He was getting the message. Too busy. Aunt Julie said she was thinking of going back to school. Besides, Mrs. Worth said to show things to his father. Fine, but Dad already knew how stupid life was.

That night, after supper, Ian cleared the plates and scraped the chunks of potato and beef and sauce globs into the bucket by the sink. They used an old two-gallon soap container for compost. He was supposed to bring it to the barn every few days and dump the garbage in the gutter. Was that wasteful? Mom said all the glop in the gutter was food for the fields. And the fields fed the cows and the cows fed them with their milk and meat. Ian loved that, A circle. Cycle. A science-book word.

But now he wondered. Were they wasting food? Could some hungry person use this stuff? Nah. Not even piggo Howie from fifth grade would eat their compost. Garbage was garbage. Why give it to somebody just because they were hungry? Why not give hungry people good food? Dad said their farm made milk enough for seventy-five families. There, that was good. He'd also heard his father say milk prices were so low they were just about giving it away. It cost more to make it than they made from it. No profit. Zilch.

Right, said Mom, and that she'd heard the definition of a lunatic is someone who repeatedly does something stupid and expects a different outcome each time. *In other words,* she told Dad in one of those nighttime fights filtering up through the hole in the floor, *in other words, we keep knocking our heads against the wall, prices already low, this stray voltage like a plague, making less and less milk, and you think somehow things will change. You're crazy!* And Dad had shouted, *Okay, you're so smart, you go ahead and change them!* Ian remembered the slam of the front door and that he had pulled a pillow over his head.

Well, Mom had changed things all right: she left. Did that help the farm? Not as far as Ian could see. If she were here, he could explain that they were doing a good thing making milk for seventy-five families for free because nationwide there was a lot of food wasted and at least they, at the Daley farm, weren't guilty of that. Okay, so nobody had to eat their garbage. Ian was relieved not to feel bad about dumping the scraps into the bucket, and the bucket into the gutter.

So, that was good. Not to feel guilty. Weird that he was taking this article so seriously. It was just a stupid homework assignment.

One night the week before, he had dinner at Keith's house.

"So, Ian, I saw your aunt Julie the other day and she said your mom's gone to see their brother, the astronomy teacher in California."

Keith shot a horrified look at his mother. Ian was more surprised by Keith's look than by hearing something he probably should have known. Shouldn't he? Wasn't California incredibly far? Was this bad news? Keith seemed to think so.

"Mom," Keith hissed at her.

Ian liked how his friend stood up for him. He hadn't said two words about his mother to Keith. Not for months now. Just "She's away" or "She's not home," exactly what he said when he answered phone calls for her. How did Keith know he couldn't say more and didn't want to discuss it?

"Can you take a message?" callers had asked at the beginning. "Tell her to call Florence." "When will she be in?" People stopped phoning when their messages weren't answered, when word got around, Ian supposed, that she was away for more than a few minutes, the evening, a day. "When will she be in?" "Pretty soon," he answered at first. Then, "I don't know." Now he thought to himself, Maybe never, and hung up. He could not say those words.

The phone didn't ring much anymore anyway.

Was this how it was, he wondered, when someone died? Gradually, if you stopped returning messages, people would get the message that you were dead. And they'd stop asking your family about you because they wouldn't want to make them feel bad.

"Ian." Keith's mother had spoken to him, softly, barely louder than his thoughts.

Ian tried to look up at her, but there were so many shades of green in the salad on his plate that he couldn't lift his eyes til he'd counted one (lettuce-leaf green), two (cucumber pale green), three (green pepper bright), four (celery, like cucumber but darker with lines).

"Don't worry. I know you tough guys hate talk like this, but I am sure that your mom loves you and doesn't want you to worry. Right?"

He had to nod yes. He wondered where Keith was. He couldn't see him across the table. His eyes were magnetized by his plate, where all the colors of green were swimming together.

One evening shortly after that dinner Aunt Julie was still in their kitchen after chores, stirring and fussing with the food she'd cooked for them instead of just leaving it in pots on the stove. She served out three plates with meatloaf, boiled buttered potatoes, and broccoli. By now, Ian had almost forgotten he hated broccoli. His mother always served him cut-up raw carrots or celery sticks instead. How could Aunt Julie be expected to know? So he ate the broccoli. Whatever. Food was food. Food was compost. Food was garbage.

But here was Aunt Julie dishing it out, sitting with them, drinking only coffee herself, fiddling with a cigarette.

"So," she started, "Warren, you got something you want to say?"

Ian's father was hunkered down, forking in food the way he shoveled corn to cows—efficient, large loads. "You go ahead."

She was mad at him, Ian could tell. She squeezed her lips together and groaned, exasperated.

"He means to tell you not to worry about your mom. She's fine, if you were wondering. Course you are." She looked at Ian. "We hear you been long-faced around town. Keith's mother and your teacher say you need to know the situation. But he"—she nodded her head at

Dad—"doesn't want you going around telling everyone your business. She's healthy and all. After New Year's she drove out to Charlie's in California and is working for a vet and going to school. And here's the new address. She said she was gonna write. Okay? So, Warren, you want to add?"

He washed his food down with milk. "You said it all." He reached for the newspaper and disappeared behind it.

Ian was so glad he hadn't walked to Barre. Neither he nor Ray reached for the address. Barre or California— what was the difference?

One afternoon last spring a man came to the farm and offered to take its picture from the air. The Daleys could buy it then, see? and they'd have a spectacular view of their beautiful place, a treasure for generations to come. Dad said, "Bull," and walked across the road to the barn. He was late for chores from talking to the power company again. Too many sick cows. Shocked or jittery. Stray voltage. Would the picture show that?

But Mom said, "Yes, I want that photo." She looked up and Ian looked up and in the streaky clouds he saw it all reflected—the farm layout. A white house to the sun side, the west, with a greening field and two brown fields edged by the winding Jiggles Brook; a red barn on the other side of a jet tail that was the road; east of the barn a jagged stretch of pasture and woods and woods and woods. Then the shapes wavered and blurred with the wind, but when the man brought the photo weeks later, Ian recognized their place immediately. Neat. Orderly. Familiar and unchanging. Dad laughed and said, "Can't see the shit pile from up that high." Mom hung the picture in the living room above the phone.

She hadn't liked how it came out. "You can't even see the home farm, or any cows. It looks dead."

"Like I said, waste of damn money," Dad said.

Ian wished he wouldn't talk like that to her. From the window over the kitchen sink he could see lights on at Aunt Julie's house. "Maybe that man took Aunt Julie's picture too, Mom. You could tape them together."

"Course he did. Whadya think?" Ray said. "He flew up the whole damn valley, stupid. He takes everyone's picture, farm, double-wide, whatever. And sells 'em to suckers like you, Ma." He put his arm around her and smiled. Only Ray could ever talk to her the way Dad did, but do it smiling and get her to smile. She liked everything about Ray, Ian figured, even his foul mouth.

"Don't call your brother stupid," she said, but she smiled as if a sucker was something she didn't mind being.

Assignment #6: World News

In March, Mrs. Worth assigned Current Events every week. They had to work harder, she said, to get ready for junior high. So many of the sixth graders wrote about the cloning of Dolly, the ewe, that Mrs. Worth read aloud sections from each paper.

Ian had written:

On Saturday, March 1, 1997 Dr. Ian Wilmut of Scotland announced the birth of the first successfully cloned mammal. They took cells from the udder of a ewe and made an exact copy of her.

The new lamb and the one they took the cells from have the same DNA like identical twins do.

I don't think they should bother cloning more animals or people because they will be wasting their money if they think a clone will be an exact copy. My mother and Aunt Julie are identical twins and boy do they act different!

Keith's said:

They cloned a sheep called Dolly to make an exact copy. Scientists did this in Scotland last week. Next I hope they clone Michael Jordan. That would be awesome to have another him. But Dennis Rodman's agent said the commissioner of basketball probably wouldn't allow them to clone Rodman!

Mrs. Worth said there was immense confusion about what the kids gleaned from the news. She decided to hold a class discussion, debate style, on the pros and cons of cloning.

What if, she asked, a couple lost their only child in a car accident? If they were unable to have other children in the usual manner, and if they did not want to adopt, should they be allowed to clone their child before he was taken off life support?

The debate was set for Monday, March 17, and Mrs. Worth arranged for the media man, Mr. Jackman, to videotape the event. She asked the students to select their positions. Not one kid elected to argue in favor of cloning. "They should adopt," a couple of kids said. "I can't, Ms. Worth. My mother says cloning is against God's will," Emily said. Even Keith had been dissuaded from his original enthusiasm when Ian explained that all clones, even Michael Jordan's, would have to start out as babies who might elect not to play sports at all.

"Okay," Mrs. Worth said finally, "I realize that the whole class is against cloning, but I think we need to examine the other side of the coin. So, I need ten volunteers ..."

No hands went up.

"Okaaay—eight."

Still no hands.

"Okaaaay. We'll try flattery. I need people who are good at arguing, lying even—people who can convince me. The kind of person who can convince me not to give homework on the weekends. The salesmen among you. The lawyers."

Most heads turned toward Keith. He covered his smiling face. Just last week he had persuaded Mrs. Worth to take back her homework assignment so that everyone could spend more time gazing at the heavens late at night with their families, beholding the comet Hale-Bopp. Keith sounded so sincere, innocent, poetic as he spoke, hands clasped to his chest, eyes lifted skyward beyond the class-room's frosty panes. "It would be more important than homework, Mrs. Worth, it would be galaxywork."

"Okay, so much for flattery," Mrs. Worth said after Keith accepted the first slot on the pro-clone team. "Now, how about bribery? Those agreeing to argue pro will have no homework this weekend except to prepare your arguments. The rest of you will have the usual boring assignments: math, spelling, language arts. Plus, each pro person will get a Snickers."

Hands shot up at that lure, and Mrs. Worth selected seven people, including Ian, whose hand was held in the air by Keith.

The weekend before the debate was particularly quiet. Dad and Ray spent both days in the sugar woods, checking lines for squirrel damage and boiling the sap that flowed from hundreds of maples into the gathering tank.

"I'll help," Ian said on Saturday morning, but Dad discouraged him, saying they had it pretty well under control. He gave Ian extra barn chores to do instead.

"I need you to do the milk dishes, wash the bulk tank, scrape and bed everyone, check Luna in the calving pen. We'll leave the cows in to save time, so you can feed extra hay at noon and grain late before milking. Set up for milking and do the calves, their milk replacer, and grain. And take it easy, watch TV or whatever. If you need anything, call Aunt Julie."

For a few moments Ian was amazed, not at the number of things on his list—things he knew anyway—but by the fact that his dad had listed them. It was the most his dad had spoken to him in months.

Ray followed Dad out the door right after breakfast, and Ian was left alone in the kitchen.

The table was loaded with cereal boxes and used bowls and cups, as well as newspapers, mail—both junk and good—and various nails, tees, washers, and the pieces of a broken waterbowl valve. Dishes and pots were jumbled in the sink.

His dad never seemed to notice things like this. Ian mentally added "clean the kitchen" to his chore list.

He started at the sink—double stainless steel. He loved double sinks. And the words *stainless steel*. The one in the milkhouse was even bigger—a long, curving tub divided in two. A wash side; a rinse side. The tiny bathroom sink by comparison seemed puny. But it was only for a single set of simple human hands, and toothpaste spit. Just one at a time in the bathroom.

From the kitchen window Ian had what his mother called the best view in the valley: their garden, the small orchard of dwarf fruit trees, a hayfield sloping to Jiggles Brook. Other fields then carried on straight to Aunt Julie's house and barn. He hadn't walked there since December, even though his buzz had grown out. He sighted the way exactly, even eyeballing the bush-hidden bend in the brook narrow enough to jump across. Ian knew where the wet spots hid under cattails, where woodchuck holes could be expected, where the pileated woodpecker might be heard and then seen knocking at the last dying elm in the valley—a great skeleton now partly blocking the home barn from Ian's view. His mother called it the home barn. She called visits to Aunt Julie "going to home."

"Is it growing up," he heard his mother ask Aunt Julie one day, "to stay so close to the nest?"

Even then he wondered whether she was speaking of herself or of Aunt Julie. They could see the home farm, walk to it easily, but Aunt Julie lived there.

Was it bad to stay close to home when you grew up?

Ian wondered again now. Was his mother just trying to leave the nest? But Dad grew up here too and he wasn't leaving. Aunt Julie didn't seem to need to go. Yet her brothers had, one to Barre and one to California. And now Mom. Why didn't she just say so and take him along? Especially to California. He didn't remember Uncle Charlie, who left when Ian was a baby. An astronomer in a college, he was probably up every night watching Hale-Bopp with a telescope. Maybe with Mom. Ian felt left out. He could understand her wanting to see someplace new. He could even understand her leaving Dad and the farm. But why didn't she take him? And why didn't she write back to him?

Forget it. These were the same questions he'd been asking for months, and he was sick of waiting for answers. He was sick of asking and being made to feel he ought to know already. Okay then, who cared? Everyone else seemed to be drifting since she left. Hurt but silent. Like big stupid dogs. Miserable but not doing anything different from always, drooling and eating and daily chores and waiting around to be kicked. Well, Ian was sick of it. He was going to forget about her. He was here because he wanted to be. Hadn't he decided to come home and not hitch to Uncle Jack's? He liked the farm, he liked the cows, he liked chores. Forget the stupid housework. He just wanted to work by himself in the barn.

Ian left the dishes in the sink and waded through mud

ruts and melting trickles in the driveway, then loped across the shiny blacktop toward the barn. He paused on the yellow line of Route 14 and looked north to Aunt Julie's mailbox on the sharp curve, where the road seemed to end; then he looked south to the Holmbergs' brick house and their barn's silver roof and several other roofs in the distance. Beyond what he could see was the turnoff for his school just before Greensbrook Center. No cars or trucks were in sight.

Ian stood at the center of the long and empty road, his feet rooted to a spot on the yellow line. His mother would freak to see him standing there. "Move!" she'd yell, all worried. But he liked the road. The sun had warmed the tar. He was at the center of the universe. He felt the vibration before a granite truck roaring south came into sight. Slowly he walked off the road, smiling.

It was then that Ian noticed a white car parked in front of the milkhouse. When had it come? Ian heard the clatter of metal as he opened the door. A red face grinned at him from behind a milk pail held high in the sunlight for scrutiny. Mr. Hutchins, milk inspector.

"Boss gone back to bed and sent you out to do the dirty work?"

"Nah," Ian said, and stopped there. He knew Mr. Hutchins was joking around and he'd heard Ray give it right back—something like "Nah, he sent me out to torch the place before the inspector leaves." But words like that didn't grow in his own mouth.

He felt shy. Yup, shy. Mom had used that word for him when he was quiet and watchful around other people. She offered it as an excuse, always sounding a little disappointed, he thought. Better to be wicked clever like Ray, he supposed. Or, better yet, to be so happy and funny the way Silas was, with laughter bubbling along like Jiggles Brook, attracting other kids to hang around and leaving the grownups behind smiling.

"Well, young fella, how's things around here? Electricity still going haywire?" Mr. Hutchins was studying the inflations. Replacing them was usually Ian's job, a tough one. You had to pull the stiff, new rubber nipples til they popped through the metal claw on the milking unit. But Ian couldn't remember the last time Mom told him to do it. That was her job. Reminding everyone. And ordering, replacing, keeping the milking equipment spiffy. Mom—slacker—gone to the sun.

"Okay, I guess," he told Mr. Hutchins. How could he describe Dad's dirty outerwear and the grit Mr. Hutchins could find in every line of Dad's hands? Dad would never pass inspection. He thought of the dishes in the sink. Their kitchen would never pass.

"Say, you don't talk much, do you? Chip off the old block."

Ian shrugged and wished he'd done the milk dishes and swept the milkhouse floor before breakfast. He suddenly wanted everything in the barn to be clean, spotless. He wanted Mr. Hutchins to pass them, to be impressed.

"Well, that's okay too." Mr. Hutchins tucked the clipboard under his arm and looked directly at Ian. "You're just a little Vermonter, aint'cha? Say, ever hear the one about President Calvin Coolidge at a White House dinner? Big, loud-talking fat lady sits by him and says, 'This is such a thrill, Mr. President. They bet me I couldn't get you to say even four words to me. Ha, ha, ha.' And Calvin Coolidge, he goes, 'Madam, you lose.'"

Ian smiled. He actually had heard that story. From Mrs. Worth, and more than once. She loved to tell it, even if at first she had to explain to some kids why it was funny. "Count the words, Avery. *Madam, you, lose.* That's three. She was bet he wouldn't say four."

Mrs. Worth appreciated quiet. She said one of her favorite quotes of all time was from Rob's father in *A Day No Pigs Would Die*, "Never overlook an opportunity to keep silent." Those words were copied and hung over the classroom drinking fountain under her other favorite quote: "Stand up for what you believe even if you're standing alone."

At the beginning of the school year Keith told Mrs. Worth the two sayings contradicted each other, and Mrs. Worth told him to think about it for the year and talk to her about it again in June. Ian liked how she didn't put him down, she just put him off.

Mr. Hutchins pushed through the swinging doors to the stable, clipboard in one hand.

Ian stayed in the milkhouse and began washing up by running steaming hot water into one side of the double sink. He didn't want to follow the inspector around. Dad always told Mom to go talk to Mr. Hutchins during inspections, said they always got a better score when she was out there being her charming self.

Ian felt helpless to charm Mr. Hutchins into overlooking the full gutters, cluttered walkways, what else? No paper towel by the sink, burned-out lightbulbs, fly spots on the pipeline, cobwebs everywhere.

Seeing their barn in his mind's eye from Mr. Hutchins's point of view, Ian figured he'd probably fail them himself.

"'Nother nail in the coffin," Dad might say when he heard that Mr. Hutchins had been around. And there would be Ray looking disgustedly at Ian, blaming him. Weren't they working hard in the woods? Couldn't Ian have cleaned up the friggin' barn?

Ian set to work like an ox after Mr. Hutchins left, even though the inspector had called out "Take it easy" to him as he tacked his report on a nail by the door. He'd gone easy on them. "Reinspect" instead of "Failed," with lots of X's showing violations. Yup—floor, walkways, lightbulbs, as well as milkstone buildup, need new inflations, hoses, and hand soap. Etc., etc. Ian felt relieved. Dad wouldn't mind about anything short of an out-and-out failure.

Still, Ian had been the one on duty, embarrassed by the inspection, and he decided to work down the list, doing what he could to correct their violations.

While he worked, he thought about the cloning debate. Chores, if you weren't rushing too much, made a good time for thinking. Ideas just fell into his brain as he swept the feed floor as if he were clearing space for them.

Ian scraped manure from under Luna. Mom's favorite cow. She had twins last spring. Bright and Beautiful, Mom named them, B&B for short. They were down in the heifer pen now. Mister, did they look different! Fraternal twins, Mom said. Bright was very black like Luna, short-legged, sway-backed. Beautiful looked like Luna's mother: tall, strong legs, straight topline, silky black and white pattern like racing clouds in a night sky. But the two calves acted just the same, as far as Ian could tell. Same slurpy way of drinking, same grunts as they ate, same way they slid their tongues up toward their nostrils. And they always stayed close to each other.

So, Mrs. Worth, who's to say what having kids with the same DNA would do for those parents? A big thing like looking alike or little things like voices and how the kids pick their noses?

Ian smiled to himself as he gathered up a soda bottle, dirty paper towels, two broken broom handles, odd scraps of wood. He replaced a grease gun and a hammer on the shelf by the breeding chart.

He dragged a long-handled shovel to the calf pens, enjoying the clean wake it left behind him. Escape route, he thought. Bright and Beautiful lay head to head with Ian's kitten curled on the hay between them. He never knew where Little Guy was anymore. Completely independent. But Ian was always glad to see him. He watched the belly rise and fall and the tips of black and white hair stick into a slant of light coming from the window behind.

The kitten had pretty much moved out here, becoming a barn cat like Chloe, Ray's big girl who was just now stepping carefully along the manure chute and into the barn. She stopped when she saw Ian and came to him, rubbing briefly against his leg. When he bent to pet her she proceeded to the sawdust pile by the wall where she pawed a hole, squatted, sniffed, and covered her turds quickly before scooting up the wall ladder into the hay mow.

Chloe was independent too, but she knew him, Ian felt sure of it. Maybe she remembered her kitty days in the house playing with him and Ray and Guernsey. She must remember her brother Guernsey. Beautiful Golden Guernsey with a soft white underbelly. The purrfect pillow pet. He remembered the night he wrote a story about Guernsey for third grade. Mom had helped him by saying, "Look at him, Ian. Look what he's doing. Write about that." Guernsey had come in quickly with a gush of cold snowy air when Mom opened the kitchen door. He had settled by the woodstove, purring so loudly Ian could almost feel the vibration through the linoleum floor.

Ian shivered. *Miss you, bud,* he told the air.

Funny how writing that story had fixed a picture in his mind. The image of Guernsey drying and purring by the stove was as clear to Ian as a movie. He could imagine Mrs. Worth's voice booming like God in the barn: "That, Master Daley, is the power of the written word!"

Before his energy for chores drained away, Ian climbed into the pen with B&B and three other heifers and began to shovel the dark slop away from their assorted resting bodies into a pile. From there he pushed it under the gate and into the gutter. B&B and Emma, also lying down, levered themselves up, dislodging Little Guy. Thelma and Louise right away came over and started to sniff the shovel and lick his jacket.

"Get outta here." Ian struck out with the shovel to scare them away so he could work. For a few seconds they cowered on the other side of the pen, but as soon as he turned his back on them and started to shove heavy manure to the gate, Bright pushed against his arm. At the same time the spray from Emma pissing on cleared cement splattered Ian's jeans.

"Damn it!" Ian shouted. He spun on them and around around in a circle, never minding that the tool had clinked hard into Emma twice; she was slower than the others to retreat. It felt good to spin around striking out, as if he were taking care of himself.

Ian clenched his teeth hard and attacked the pile again, but the heifers walked through it, bumping him again in their confusion.

"Friggin' idiots, damn britches," Ian muttered, borrowing Dad's words and Ray's and slapping the animals again.

The wad he was pushing against was heavy. The shovel that his father wielded with such ease wasn't doing its job. He'd cleaned half the pen, but the pile wouldn't slide under the gate. He was hot, his coat was too heavy, and suddenly he felt the futility of the task. The mess he was trying to move was making fun of him, grunting in Ray's voice: *What a wimp.*

"Shit, shit!" Ian yelled, and he kicked once at retreating Thelma. He cracked the battered shovel against the bars of the pen, hurting his own hands. He shoved it, javelin-like, out of the pen to the walkway beyond, where it clattered, bounced once, and lay still.

Ian climbed over the pile of manure and out the gate, pulling it shut with a bang. He threw himself onto the first soft, clean place he could find: the old hay swept into a pile at the end of the feed floor.

He lay panting, whistling mad air through his teeth along with a hissed repetition of every bad barn word he'd heard: *bitch, whore, retard, stupid friggin' shitbag moron idiot idiot idiot.* Just like Dad.

Then he stopped. That was it. He just lay face down, exhausted, out of steam. Out of steam. Now he felt weak and small. Ray was right. He was a wimp. Undone by a single heifer pen. If his father acted like this, nothing would ever get done. Sure, he hollered and cursed, but he didn't flop down in front of the cows' noses and cry. Ray neither.

Then Ian did start crying. He heard cow breath and neckchain rattle close to his ears, and the sounds made him cry harder even as he rolled over and looked up into the big floppy underchin of Joan and saw Beryl's enormous dark eyes close to his own. Her breath came as a huge sigh, as if she were fed up with him.

He started a painful laugh. "I'm on your plate, girls," he said to them. He lay back, suddenly feeling cradled by the hay, safe. Joan's sandpaper tongue rasped against his damp ear and cheek. And again. Then she stretched her big head over his for a bite of hay.

That Monday Ian stayed home from school in bed. No one knew. Ray had dashed in from chores, ran a shower, banged bowls and cupboards, crinkled cereal boxes, and dashed out, yelling, "Ian! Seven o'clock! Move it!" The truck started and rattled out the driveway.

Ian lay on his back, took a deep breath, and watched the covers pulled tight to his chin rise and then sink.

Next he lifted one thumb from his side just high

enough to make the quilt rise, a tiny little tent. He relaxed his hand. The quilt felt warm and snug but incredibly heavy.

He flexed his feet and wiggled his toes. The calm surface at the foot of his bed jumped. He stopped. And wiggled again. And could almost feel a kitten pouncing on his jiggling undercover feet with pin-sharp claws poking through. But Little Guy would be in the barn. Ian quickly pulled up his feet and curled on his side into a ball.

When his father and Aunt Julie came in for breakfast two hours later, Ian heard their voices. They thought he was at school—that is, if they thought of him at all. He lay very still so as not to creak the bed. Stiller than sleep. He took very thin, quiet breaths. He was amazed at how still he could be. Almost dead.

"So, Warren, scrambled or fried?" Aunt Julie sounded tired.

"Don't matter. I ain't hungry," Dad grumbled in his bear voice.

"Jeez, that's a first." She was trying to joke. Uh-oh, Aunt Julie, thought Ian.

"Oh yeah? Whyn't you go on home. I 'preciate your help and all, but I ain't gonna sit cheery playing restaurant."

"Don't go yelling at me, Warren. You been taking my help. You need it and that's fine. No one says you got to be cheery. I know it was another shitty morning in that electric-shock-therapy barn of yours, but don't take it out on me."

"Sound more like your sister all the time. Push, push, when a guy's down."

"Holy Mother of God, you think you're the only one down. You drive Mariette away. You work Ray like an ox. You never even notice the little kid. And you yell at me for cooking your damned breakfast after washing your milk dishes and scraping your shitty cows!"

Ian heard things crashing to the floor, a loud slam and rustle of paper, the phone dropped, then his Dad's voice unbearably hard and tight like a fist in the air.

Harry? Warren Daley.

Yeah, well, I got a herd for you.

Uh-uh, your place. Who's gonna come here? Get zapped.

Why should I be sick of it? Maybe I'm getting cured finally.

Soon as you can. Take a look.

A good herd? Used to be.

Okay then.

The phone clicked quietly. Ian couldn't hear Aunt Julie, wasn't sure she was still there, it was so quiet.

"Now you think I could eat by myself? I would really appreciate it."

Ian heard the fridge open and the whoosh of a can being opened. The front door clicked.

Ian couldn't help himself jumping quietly as a cat out of bed and hurrying to the window to watch for Aunt

Julie. Her head was bent to the March wind and her red hair whipped all over crazily as she ducked into her car and drove away. He wished she'd come back. Ian felt trapped. Why? Why hadn't he gone to school?

He had just felt too still to get up, not tired exactly, just motionless. That stillness where he breathed lightly and watched his tiny undercover movements with surprise had not been unpleasant. Like he'd be a picture on the wall for a while, not a movie. It felt nice, restful really, to take a place in the background.

But now that calm was gone. In its place was fear, maybe how a trapped raccoon feels before the trapper shows up. Ian didn't know exactly who or what to be afraid of. After all, he wasn't hurt, just stuck. Alone with Dad. He wished someone would tell him what to do.

If he went downstairs, what would happen? Would Dad yell, or do something worse to him? Dad never had. Mostly just ignored him.

Ian eased back to his bed, trying hard not to creak the frame or floorboards. Of course if his Dad heard him and came up to his room, he could say he was sick. That was so easy. Why hadn't he thought of it? Why worry at all? His dad wouldn't know he was never sick.

He heard the refrigerator close again. Another whoosh and snap of a can being opened.

Mrs. Worth and Officer Austin had taught DARE to Ian's class in the fall. He'd thought about his dad's drinking, his mom's coffee, Aunt Julie's smoking. A few times he'd wondered if all the problems people were supposed to suffer from those things applied to his family.

"How do you tell if someone has a problem with drugs?" he'd asked his mother in the barn one afternoon when Dad and Ray were still chopping corn.

"What drugs?" She looked up at him over the grain cart.

"Anything, like, you know, nicotine or caffeine, or alcohol."

"Jeez, Ian, I thought you meant like *drug* drugs. Why? Who's got a problem?"

"I don't know, just wondering."

She stopped scooping grain and looked straight at him. "You'd know," she said. "They'd act funny, different. They wouldn't be like the person you always knew. They'd act weird, sick. Granpa Daley drank. And Uncle Fred. He'd get so he'd be funny, teasing you kids, telling really gross jokes. Then he'd get mean and hit Julie. He had a problem. But a few beers, cups of coffee, for chrissake, a few cigarettes, Ian, that's life. You worry too much."

Ian crept downstairs to see if his father looked different. Dad stood at the kitchen sink with his back turned, facing out the window. Ian knew the view he was seeing. Was the bluebird there? Was Chloe walking up from Jiggles Brook through the corn stubble? Were the wild turkeys grazing there? Was there smoke rising from Aunt Julie's chimney?

Ian waited at the foot of the stairs, unsure. He realized he could cross the living room and go all the way out the front door and Dad probably wouldn't notice. Dad was standing there, but he was far away. His shoulders were rounded, his dark hair lay flat on one side, all messed up on the other, some bits of hay stuck out just begging to be removed the way Mom used to do. Ian bet his dad hadn't combed his hair since she left. He was surprised Aunt Julie let him get like this. She was a hairdresser, for chrissake.

Dad leaned against the sink, his arms supporting him on either side, the fingers of his right hand just touching the beer can on the counter. They rubbed lightly, without sound, his only movement, only sign of life.

Ian hadn't come down to escape. He wanted his dad's smell, his bulk, his heat. He wanted his dad to turn around and notice him. From his station at the foot of the stairs, Ian stared at the broad back framed through the kitchen doorway, the scratchy, sticking-out hair, the torn shirt straining over those big shoulders, and he wished he could go to him and touch his arm and turn himself in. *Hey, Dad? It's me.*

Just then Dad's hand twitched, knocking the can, then steadying it, trying to field the drops that splashed out. He spotted Ian.

"What the ... Ian, you scared the bejesus out of me! What are you doing here?"

Ian walked to the stool at the kitchen counter, suddenly planless, speechless. He sat. "Sorry," he said.

"Where'd you come from? They bring you home? You sick?" His father was asking these things, but Ian could tell he was still far away, his eyes clouded. He might as well be gazing still out that window, lost so deep in himself he wouldn't hear any answer; hardly heard his own questions.

"Yeah," Ian said, "they brought me home." You idiot, he wanted to say. Who the hell is "they"? His father wouldn't even know the name of anyone at school. Mrs. Pickle brought me. Mr. Baboon drove me. Didn't he see that Ian had his damn pajamas on?

"Okay. Well. You wanna go lie down? What's it? Your gut? Your head?"

"Both, I guess. I'll just sit." Ian sat at the kitchen counter, unable to think what to do next. Looked at Dad and waited.

"Yeah. Well, you better rest or something. Know something? I'm kinda beat myself. I'm gonna just lie on the sofa here a little while. You okay? Good. Okay then."

Dad crossed heavily into the living room and settled like a wet bale onto the sagging sofa. He curled onto his side, his back to Ian once again. Startling white skin showed through holes in the soles of both dark socks, one gray, one blue. Asleep or not, he was gone.

Ian's chest hurt. He forced out a piece of sound in there, a tiny, high whimper, just one, but Dad never heard, or if he did he never said anything.

Ian was suddenly freezing in spite of the March sun outside and the ice that dripped from the roof as evidence of thaw. He put his hand on the woodstove. Cold. That scared him.

He looked around the room for something warm. Made his eyes skip over the sofa. He picked up Mom's afghan, shaggy with cat hair, from the arm of the rocking chair, wrapped it around himself, and curled up on the braided rug next to the sofa where Dad would have to step on him when he got up. Dust no one had vacuumed or swept in months puffed up in front of Ian's eyes. He closed them and made himself go to sleep.

Ian hadn't missed the cloning debate; they had waited for him. Too bad. He told himself he didn't care, not even about the Snickers. What was cloning to him? He couldn't think of anyone he would want to clone, not even himself. The twins he knew, his mother and aunt, had no benefit from being clones as far as he was concerned. Just confusing. Nothing but extra trouble.

Still, Ian was glad to be back at school. His day with his father gained him only a stiff neck from sleeping on the drafty floor. And it let him see Dad as sad, not just grouchy. Great. Now they had something in common, the same personal news. Misery loves company. Heartbreaking, huh?

As he entered the crowded sixth-grade room, picked up his backpack, and kicked Keith's under his desk, he felt more at home than at home.

"Move the desks to the sides and let's have only chairs facing each other in two rows—Pros here and Cons facing them over here. Hurry up now, let's get to the good part." Mrs. Worth was rubbing her hands together, probably to drum up the excitement she wanted them to feel.

Ian plunged into this simple chore, the general shuffling and banging. He moved his desk and several others. As far as he was concerned, this was the good part. So easy here to be in on things. Nothing hard or lonely. You just followed along.

Amos found he could get a certain squeal from the old linoleum by scraping his sneaker, wet from the muddy playground, just so. He did it three times before Mrs. Worth said with a sigh, "Enough, Mr. Audette. Where should you be? Con. Of course, Master Con-Man Audette."

Ian sat with the small Pro group. "Think about it," Mrs. Worth said to them, plucking Ian from his daydreams and Keith and Silas from their fooling. "Imagine you *are* pro-cloning. You're playing a role here, using your brains to figure out how someone else might think. Stretch yourself. Open your mind. No one is going to report you to the anti-cloning activists. Don't worry your conservative little hearts."

Ian forgot his ideas about twins. The only thing the discussion made him think of today was his dead cat Guernsey, his first, the one he loved the best. The coydogs had been yipping recent nights. If they had only left him a piece of Guernsey, a bone or claw or piece of orange fluff, maybe he would want to clone him. But it all seemed so ridiculous. What's gone is gone, he thought.

He sat shoulder to shoulder with Keith, a gap between his chair and Sarah's, facing the two rows of smug-looking Cons.

He sighed and looked at the clock. Only 12:30. Two hours and forty minutes til bus time. He began to wish the day were over. Not school, but the whole day. He felt the emptiness of home tugging and worrying him. Here at least he could glide. He knew what to do and what to expect. He could listen and wait for time to pass.

Sarah sneezed and said, "Excuse me."

He wondered if she noticed that the whole sixth-grade room smelled like his socks. Sweaty and sickening. He wondered what hers smelled like and took a quick glance at her feet: black-and-white Adidas hooked on the front rung of her chair. Amazing shoes. Clean, and the laces threaded every hole and were tied! Ian almost laughed, something that felt very odd. Why had he never noticed her feet before? He looked at Keith's and at his own. Keith was actually wearing what might at one time have been the same style as Sarah's, but now—transformed. Keith was night and Sarah was day. Keith's laces, if you could call the muddy, frayed strips laces, entered only the two lowermost holes. The long pieces that remained encircled the whole of his shoes under and over several times and were tied in a major multiple unbreakable knot over the arch. The lace structure was further held in place by an inch or so of mud that encased most of both shoes.

Keith, Ian knew, never tied or untied his shoes. Pull on, kick off, that was the way. Ian's own Converses were unimpressive. Just some mud. Torn on one side. Big. Cloddy, like every pair of footwear in the Daleys' mudroom, his, Ray's, Dad's, even Mom's, all looking alike. Dark, mud-filmed or caked. Misshapen or flattened, all roughly the same size, 8-11. He wondered what Mom wore now, in California.

Ian looked again at Sarah's small, tucked neatness. He sighed, vaguely feeling something new to worry about.

The cloning debate carried on without his even noticing.

Assignment #7: Universal News

For the next three weeks chaos filled the
Daley farm. Phone calls about cows rang in
at all hours. Mr. Henry, the auctioneer, hung
around, taking notes, inspecting equipment,
arranging to truck everything to his sale barn.
Aunt Julie tried to reason with Dad. "Wait,"
she said, "just wait." Dad continued running
down his list: call vet, look up breeding dates,
cull Alma.

One morning at breakfast Ray, looking
jumpy, finally said the unspeakable: "What
would Mom say? You can't do this and not
even tell her!" To which Dad replied, "I'd tell
her if she was in hearing range."

Ian drifted. After his day playing hookey
he decided school was his best, simplest
option, so he went. But he stopped doing
homework. At home he spent most of his
time in the barn. The sun was thin and he felt
warmer there. Besides, he had to do a lot of
chores. His father spent more and more time

in the sugarhouse, cleaning up or just sitting, Ray said. But when he came down to the barn after Ray, with Ian's help, had finished milking, he seemed calm. At supper, he sometimes smiled. Once when Ian poured milk for everyone Dad cleared his throat and said, "Thanks. Say, over two hundred gallons grade A so far this year!"

One night Ian went out late to check the cows about to freshen, feed hay, and turn off the lights. Luna was due, and he and Ray had moved her that afternoon to the calving pen. Ian had asked Ray, "Think Mom remembers when Luna's due?" but Ray had shrugged.

"Probably," he said finally.

"We should let her know if it's a heifer," Ian said.

Ray shrugged again and looked at Ian as though he were something pitiful. "Ian, you got to stop thinking about her."

"Don't you?"

He rubbed Luna's head. "I called her once at Uncle Jack's. She sounded like she wasn't there. Said she was tired. Never asked about the farm. I just think we should tell her Dad's selling the cows, but I don't guess it would make any difference. If she cared she wouldn't have left."

"She cared."

Ray sighed. "Forget about it. We're doing okay."

"What about without the cows? What will we do all the time, what will Dad do?"

"Cut wood. Hay. I don't know." He started down the

long aisle of the barn, away from Ian. "I'm going to take the electricians' course at the the voc center and figure out this voltage thing. Then we can start up again, sometime."

Ian was amazed at his brother. They never talked. He had no idea that Ray contained such plans, such hope for the farm with no hope for Mom.

That night Ian checked the dim corner pen where Luna lay chewing calmly, seemingly untroubled by her swollen udder and bulging belly. Ian spread fresh hay by her head, squatted down, and watched her sniff it and scoop a mouthful with her tongue. The crooked white marking on her nose made her look like a clown. A cow clown. Ian smiled at her. No wonder Mom had liked her so much. He checked her butt again. No feet showing yet. Her vulva was large and soft velvety dark. She lumbered heavily to standing, then shuffled and hunched, squeezing out just little dribs and drabs of manure. Soon. Ian knew the signs. He spoke softly to her and stroked under her chin until she stretched her neck long and closed her eyes. He brought her more hay, and a pail of water so she wouldn't have to get zapped drinking from the metal water bowl. Then he made a bed for himself of the old hay outside the calving pen so he could sleep in the barn that night.

He woke to the sound of Luna's neckchain jangling and her front hooves pawing the floor of the pen. Her breath came in short snorts. A wet head and two front hooves flapped from her tail end; Ian climbed over the side of the pen just in time to ease the slippery calf to the floor. He wiped off its muzzle and tickled each nostril with a stalk of hay until the calf sneezed and shook its head. As he tugged it toward Luna's searching lowing head, he moved its rear legs apart, checking.

"Bull." Dad appeared on the other side of the gate draped in milking hoses and pails. "Just as well."

His turn or not, Ian put one more envelope in the mailbox for his mother. Mailbox. Malebox. Only boys here now, he thought. First time he ever sent any message so far as California. He hoped it would shock her even from this distance:

First you left.
Now the cows—April 11.
Even Luna.
She had a bull anyway.

Two nights before the cows were due to be trucked to the auction barn, Ian looked out his open window at the night sky and tried to figure out where the comet would be. "I don't know," he muttered, frustrated. Ian thought it had come and gone, old news. But no, Mrs. Worth was hooked on Hale-Bopp. They were all supposed to write this month about Hale-Bopp, either a regular Current Events article or an eyewitness account.

They didn't seem to be getting the paper at the Daley farm this month and you just couldn't question Dad these days about anything. Ian could understand not wanting any questions. "I don't know" was what Ian himself said these days when Mrs. Worth asked him what he thought. Ian wasn't afraid of Dad now, not since he'd seen him curled up on the sofa like a baby bear; he just didn't want to bother him.

He'd noticed a weird thing that afternoon from this very window. A car pulled in across the road. Surprise. Mrs. Worth got out and went right in the milkhouse door. She never even glanced at the house. She seemed to know where she was going as if she knew it was choretime and she'd arrived to help. Funny. Mrs. Worth, the hired hand. Only she was still wearing her dress from school. And sneakers. Like she always did. In case she had to make a quick getaway, she told the sixth graders. If she was coming to complain about his work, fine. He was glad because he knew she wouldn't get far talking to Dad, or Ray, who was probably the only one in the barn anyway. The phone rang then, something about the auction, and Ian almost forgot about Mrs. Worth til now.

It was cold out for April, but Ian guessed he'd better look for the stupid comet. He sure wasn't going to get up at two in the morning to look. He couldn't see the northwestern sky from his room, which faced east toward the barn, and northwest was supposed to be the place. But Ian figured if it was as big and impressive as Mrs. Worth said, then he might catch a glimpse of the tails at least, and sooner than two a.m. He'd look for a while; if he didn't see anything he'd write that no comet was visible from his house. He was getting tired of these stupid assignments anyway. It was just as well they weren't getting the paper anymore. Who cared about all that garbage. It never told him any of the stuff he really wanted to know. Like what was going to happen after the cows left? What would his dad do besides drink? Where did Ray drive off to after supper so he wasn't home even now at midnight? What was Ian supposed to do without the girls? His whole day revolved around the cows and their needs. Without chores there would be only school, and an empty barn, and that was a scary thought.

Looking at the sky was not going to answer his questions, so he pulled his head in and scooped up Little Guy. The cat had strolled over from the barn with Ian after chores as if he sensed change. Exhausted from chasing his tail, he'd been lying at Ian's feet. Ian turned off the light and went to bed.

Little Guy's scratching woke Ian from a restless sleep. He felt weight on his leg and sat up grabbing for the kitten. He could see nothing at first in the darkness but a shadow jumping off the bed. What was it then that seemed to fill the room?

Cold, for one thing. He had left the window open and was freezing from the April chill. No wonder he wasn't sleeping well. He wanted only to burrow back under his quilt and hide from whatever was out there. Let Dad deal with it, or Ray. He must be home by now. His truck should be in the driveway. Ian dragged himself out of bed. He should at least check on Ray and close the window.

No Ranger, only Dad's old farm truck over by the barn. And what looked like a wobbly light in the milkhouse. That was funny. After dinner he had watched Ray go across the road to check on Luna, whose occasional moan of missing her calf sounded deeply from within the barn. Ian had seen the lights go out before Ray drove off. Was Dad up already? Was that a flashlight moving around? Maybe the power was off. Was it morning already?

Then Ian sniffed and knew. He whimpered and tugged the window closed. He smelled smoke; that wavery light must be fire, and he didn't know what to do. More than anything he wanted to go back to bed and wake up on a different day at a different place where this wasn't happening. But he couldn't sleep through this nightmare. *Fire and barns don't mix.* How many times had he heard that?

"Dad!" he yelled, pulling open his door and running down the hall. As he grabbed the doorknob of his parents' room and shouted again, "Dad! Mom! I smell smoke! I think there's fire in the milkhouse!" he suddenly began to doubt what he had seen, and to feel foolish. He was glad to find the room empty, the bed shadowy with disheveled blankets. He felt a wash of relief.

He knows, Ian thought. He's already out there. Ian's breath came easier. It's okay. It's okay. It's not all up to me. Calling Mom—God, that was dumb. Why did I do that?

Ian shook his head, wide awake now. He knew he had to go out there and do what he could to help, but without panic now, he took time to dress quickly. As he came off the stairs and crossed the living room he could see through the windows the glowing, staggering light, bigger now, in the milkhouse across the road.

Where was Dad? And Ray? Had Dad called the fire department? Dad was in the department, for chrissake. Even if he didn't go to many meetings, he would know to call the others for help. Ian pulled on his boots and coat and let Little Guy, scratching at the door, race out into the night ahead of him. Safer on his own, Ian figured, out of the buildings, away from him. No cat should trust a Daley to keep it safe.

He thought of the cows. How would they get them out? Had his dad started? Now that Ian was near the barn he heard mooing and the clinking of chains. The milkhouse door was smoking; he was afraid to open it. He ran around to the side door near the manure chute and almost tripped on Dad, slouched on the ground by the open door.

"Dad," Ian breathed. "The fire . . . what happened?"

"Whoa." His father grabbed for Ian's ankle. Ian knew something was very wrong.

"Are you okay?" he said, thinking, Smoke, smoke, he's sick from smoke. Smoked like bees in a hive and all dopey. Ian pulled his foot away and tried to look at both his father and the cows at once. He could see nothing clearly. His father's face lay in deep shadow; the interior of the barn was a blur of restless movement and jittery sound. Luna's call raised in pitch to a shriek.

"Close the door, boy, go back a bed." Dad's voice was slow and too calm. Was he crazy?

"Dad, we got to get the cows." But even as Ian spoke he started to cry, feeling helpless. The smoke thickened, the crackling sound grew. His stupid father lay there.

"Let 'em go, let 'em go," Dad was crooning. Then he sat bolt upright and clenched Ian's whole leg hard, hugging it and gushing in a voice unlike any Ian had ever heard, "My boy, you're a good boy." Then Dad pushed him away from the door so hard Ian was tossed into the air flying and rammed breathless into night-hardened mud. "Get the hell out of here. Go to Julie's or I'll throw you there."

Ian's body hit with a thud. Stunned with the force that knocked him down, he stopped crying. He wasn't scared of the old man lying on the ground so much as of the smoke filling the barn and of the sound of fire crackling.

"You're crazy, Dad, we got to get the cows out. Get up!

Get out of the way." Ian moved too fast then for Dad, a stumbling blockade, to grab him. "Dad, they're our cows!"

Instead of trying for the door and the wrenching sound of the cows, Ian ran faster than he ever had to the house, to the kitchen, to the phone. He called the number on the frayed sticker stuck to the receiver, told the dispatcher to hurry, really hurry to the Daley farm, fire in the barn. He hung up and called Aunt Julie, whose voice quickly lost its sleepiness when she heard him.

"I'm coming. Don't go into that barn!" she shouted.

He hung up, not wanting to hear her last words. He raced across the road again, around to the back of the barn, and met a group of confused cows, released from their chains and unsure whether to huddle near their smoking home or head uphill toward the woods. He heard Dad's voice, hoarse but loud from within, "Ian, just chase 'em from the door, don't come in here, don't."

Ian had a job then. It was work enough for one person to flag and wave and dodge around the panicked cows, trying to calm them with his voice even as he herded them toward the dark but safe hillside.

At some point sirens sounded, and others arrived. A circle of neighbors joined him. Men he knew directed him and the cows with calm authority. If this was new to them or frightening, Ian would never have guessed it. If he couldn't see flames spreading now to the haymow, Ian would have enjoyed the incredible night out, safe on the hillside with strong neighbors who knew what they were doing. Tucked under his worry for the barn, the cows, the cats, and his father was the knowledge that he had said *Get up* and Dad got up. He hadn't totally given up, a drunken dragon lying by the door.

Later, like a dream, he remembered a flash in the sky right there above Aunt Julie's in the northwest sky. It was the most wonderful thing he had ever seen. A sign in the sky. Vision of light, glowing fireball of gases and tail of ice. All the things Mrs. Worth told them about its science made it bigger and more powerful to him. He caught his breath and laughed at himself in spite of the confusion around him. Others were pointing. In the calm after the fire was out, people stood around in the chill drinking coffee. Someone handed him a cup of hot chocolate. Aunt Julie was saying, "I heard Charger barking. Thought it was just the comet, he's been barking at the comet. I was almost asleep when Ian called."

How many light-years away? That meant it wasn't really there at that moment. Its image was above the smoke in the sky. The brightest spirit. A brilliant head and a tail. Mrs. Worth said twin tails, but Ian saw only one. *Whoosh.* It was enough. He vowed to watch for it every night it was visible.

As the night ended and the sun began to reveal the mess left of the barn, Aunt Julie grabbed him and hung on so tightly he couldn't move, and gave up trying. He let himself be led across the road. When he awoke later, he was in his own bed. It was light, and his father, filthy and smelling of smoke, snored in a chair by his side clutching Ian's old quilt in his huge hands.

The next few days passed in a blur. Jolted by disaster into action, Aunt Julie convinced Dad that the fire was a blessing in disguise. They could cull the sickest cows and move the rest to the smaller home farm, where stray voltage wouldn't plague them. It was so close. Why, maybe she might want to switch houses eventually. She had no use for a barn anyway, and the roadside location would be good for her business. They could add on if it wasn't big enough. Why hadn't she thought of it before?

Of course it wasn't so simply done, but that was what happened.

The fire investigators said it looked like arson, common along that road, oily rags in the milkhouse. The worst damage was there. A few cows were sickened beyond cure by smoke, but most escaped, including Luna, who tolerated Ian's hugs with great patience.

Aunt Julie's milkhouse was smaller and more old-fashioned but in good shape. She had never gotten rid of the bulk tank, since the milkhouse was built around it. For now, Ian, Ray, and Dad walked or drove to do chores. Maybe they would move there during the summer.

Ray, it turned out, had spent the night with Uncle Jack in Barre. Said he didn't know where else to go. He told Ian he'd had a fight with Dad. About selling the cows, about not telling Mom. Mrs. Worth had walked in on their argument. She just wanted to talk to Dad sometime, she said, about Ian, about a job she wanted to get him for the summer, working for her daughter, the vet. If Ian could just keep up his grades; they were slipping lately. After she left, Dad told Ray he was going to torch the place and put an end to the farm once and for all. "You boys will be better off," he'd told him.

Ray said, "At Uncle Jack's we called Mom to let her know how crazy Dad was, but I didn't think he'd really do it. Know what she said? From way out in California? 'Oh, Ray! Look at the sky tonight. That comet is the most gorgeous thing. Don't worry about your father. He'll figure something out.' That's what she said. And that she's in school. And that I should ... well ... nothing."

Little Guy. The night of the fire, by the side of the road in front of the house he lay dead. Hit by some vehicle. Ray found him and said he would do the burying, that Ian shouldn't look, it was bad.

Ian said, "Please don't bury his collar." But he felt okay. At least the coydogs didn't get Little Guy. At least it wasn't a mystery. What Ian always minded most before with the missing cats was not knowing for sure what had happened.

Ian kept the red collar on his desk. He missed the little guy. He tried to write a poem for him, but all he put down was:

Goodbye
Little Guy.

He taped it to the wall above his desk. The collar was his memento. It hardly seemed red, it was so fuzzy with black fur. DNA, for cloning, Ian figured. If science ever progressed that far he'd learn more about it and maybe have it done.

In the meantime, he kept his vow to look for Hale-Bopp every night. In the hours he spent outside gazing at the sky, especially that magical northwestern part above the home farm, he remembered that looking up always made him feel better. The blaze in the sky seemed a messenger from another time, visible now, but already long gone. Saying, *I'm gone, I'm here at the same time!* Sometimes, after chores, his whole family looked up before the men started the walk home. Of course no one spoke; that was fine with him.

Assignment #8: Anything

HALE-BOPP'S SHOW SINKING
ON THE HORIZON

*I read an article about Hale-Bopp concluding its
spectacular show by the end of this month and how
it will not come again for 2,400 years. It is already
150 million miles away.*

*But the moon will be full the night of May 21
so some bright things stay the same.*

*With Hale-Bopp fading I have made my
decision. I won't clone Little Guy from the fur on
his collar even if it could be done and I wouldn't
even clone Guernsey if I had some of his DNA. I
will bury the collar.*

*I know it could be done if not today then when
I grow up. I could just keep the collar and the hairs
and someday I could have an exact replica of my
little guy.*

*But exact is never exactly the same and for
now I go along with saying goodbye.*

Ian took the collar to the sugar woods. The ground was finally soft without oozing mud and he dug a deep hole. In it he put the red collar and the little poem to which he had added: *I loved you a great deal.* He filled in the hole and went to do his chores.

That night, Ian wrote his mother a letter, again out of turn, but he was feeling generous:

By the time June first swings by, which as you know is my birthday, I may have a summer job working for Dr. Worth. I hear you work for a vet so we might have something in common. If you are thinking about a present, no kittens, please. I'm not ready. But when I am I think I'll call it Hale-Bopp to keep us company when the comet is gone or rather when we can't see it any more. When you were gone, I didn't know why and that was a bad feeling. I am happy to know that you are ok. If you want to send a present, please send money so I can get a good bike like Keith's. I want to ride with the guys and just to the store and places and it will be a while before we can get our licenses. But not that long.

Love, Ian

Ian started the journal that Mrs. Worth suggested all junior high schoolers would need:

May 21, 1997: Tonight is the full moon and with all that light filling the night sky you can hardly make out old H-B's tail at all. But I know it's there.

Goodbye Hale-Bopp, I'll be missing you. If a kitten has your name, don't worry. He'll be small and warm and furry and he'll chase his tail and sleep on my bed when he feels like it. Not like you, so far away and huge with your icy tail streaming behind you. You were around all spring and I was too lazy to look for you. Now I won't see you but I know you are there somewhere.

Goodbye.

Finally, in June, Ian got a note from his mother. The card was a picture of a sunset over the Pacific, and a check slid out as Ian read:

Oh Ian, my baby, Happy Birthday!
My heart is breaking from how much
I have hurt you
by leaving.

It was never you,
it was your dad
and the farm
I couldn't bear
anymore.

I have gone
back to study

at Uncle Charles's
college.

I always liked
science.

If I learn enough,
earn enough,
I can
send for you.

But I know you are fine,
my wonderful son.

Ian cried when he read this but then thought, She wrote, good, that's an improvement. He knew he would write back. He didn't know what he would say, but he would sign it:

I,
A baby?
No way!